Henry George Tomkins

The Life and Times of Joseph in the Light of Egyptian Lore

Henry George Tomkins

The Life and Times of Joseph in the Light of Egyptian Lore

ISBN/EAN: 9783337329990

Printed in Europe, USA, Canada, Australia, Japan

Cover: Foto ©Andreas Hilbeck / pixelio.de

More available books at **www.hansebooks.com**

𝔅𝔶-𝔓𝔞𝔱𝔥𝔰 𝔬𝔣 𝔅𝔦𝔟𝔩𝔢 𝔎𝔫𝔬𝔴𝔩𝔢𝔡𝔤𝔢

XVII

THE

LIFE AND TIMES OF JOSEPH

IN THE LIGHT OF EGYPTIAN LORE

BY THE

REV. H. G. TOMKINS

LATE VICAR OF BRANSCOMBE
AUTHOR OF 'STUDIES ON THE TIMES OF ABRAHAM,' ETC.

SECOND EDITION

FLEMING H. REVELL COMPANY

NEW YORK | CHICAGO
112 FIFTH AVENUE | 148 & 150 MADISON STREET

The Religious Tract Society London

PREFACE.

IN this little book the reader will find himself out of the high-road of Biblical exposition, and (in conformity with the general title of this Series of Handbooks) in By-paths of Bible Knowledge.

With questions of textual criticism I have not been concerned. The date and origin and authorship of those documents which may have been used in the writing, or subsequent redaction, of the Book of Genesis, are not the matters which lay in my way. But, quite apart from all such studies, it is surely a very interesting and instructive thing to lay the narrative as it stands side by side with the daily increasing information which comes to the student of Egyptian lore, and of other branches of Biblical archaeology.

This I had done in concise form with regard to the Life of Joseph in a paper which may be found in the *Transactions of the Victoria Institute* for 1880[1]; and I have since studied, as far as I am aware, all that has been written by Egyptologists bearing on the subject.

The references in the following pages, and a few

---

[1] Vol. XV, pp. 83 *et seqq.*

notes by way of Appendix, will guide the reader to
the more important sources of information. The very
able work of Dr. de Cara, of Rome, on the Hyksôs[1],
has added the latest digest of information with regard
to this obscure but most attractive period of history;
and I would also draw special attention to the fine
Memoir on Bubastis by M. Naville, as well as his
volume on Goshen, both of them published by the
Egypt Exploration Committee.

The narrative of the life of Joseph in the Book of
Genesis has been treated in the most thoughtful,
learned, and devout manner by the venerable Franz
Delitzsch in his *New Commentary on Genesis*, of which
an English translation (with 'numerous improvements
and additions' by the author) is available for those who
do not read German[2].

For an able and candid exposition of the conserva-
tive views of the Biblical text, I would refer to *The
Foundations of the Bible*, by my friend Canon R. H.
Girdlestone[3], and especially, as bearing on my own
subject, to p. 46, and the close of the work, and the
valuable chapter on Hebrew Spelling. And for a more
popular view of the same general subject it is very
well to read the same author's small and handy tract,
*The Age and Trustworthiness of the Old Testament
Scriptures*.

For my own part I think it right to reiterate the
belief that what have been called 'precritical' studies

[1] *Gli Hyksôs, &c.*, del P. Cesare A. de Cara, Roma, 1889.
[2] Clark, Edinburgh, 1889.   [3] Eyre and Spottiswoode, 1890.

in the way of collation of the Scripture narrative as it stands, with all that becomes known from monumental sources (as they are now generally called), are of a very high rank of importance and value ; and provide us, indeed, with most valuable material (as, for instance, with palaeographic data, and other kindred details) bearing on the more mature decisions of what is exclusively called ' criticism.'

A very striking instance of an attempt to disprove the early date of the Egyptian narratives of the Book of Genesis is given in an Appendix at the end of this volume, and previously in a letter by myself in the *Academy* for Jan. 31, 1891, to which no reply has been sent. In this case the structure of such names as Potiphar and Potiphera is alleged to prove a late date, no earlier than the ninth century B.C. But the allegation itself is an unaccountable error.

So much it has seemed right to say. For some one might easily object to anything written with regard to Joseph which does not first disprove the floating objections to the narrative of Holy Scripture.

With regard to the spelling of proper names, I have tried to indicate the difference between the mere aspirate and the guttural sound indicated by *Kh,* as in Haran and Kharran, for instance ; and between the Hebrew letters *Kaph* and *Kheth,* as in Shekem instead of Shechem. But I could not venture on Khebron for Hebron, and the like, for reasons which may easily be supplied.

CONTENTS.

———

CHAPTER I.

WHEN Abram, at the call of God, had journeyed from Ur of the Chaldees west on his way to the place which Jehovah should show him, he halted on the east of the great river until the death of Terakh, his father. The region was called Padan-Aram, and its capital was Kharran, which took its name in the old pre-Semitic language from its being a great halting-place on the high-road of war and commerce between the Euphrates and the Nile. The name itself means 'road.'

When Abram had departed to the Land of Promise, Nakhor, his brother, with his wife Milkah and their house, had remained, and Kharran is called 'the city of Nahor' in the narrative of Eliezer's mission. There God gave Rachel to Jacob, as He had given Rebekah to his father, and there Jacob served the seven years which were in his eyes 'but a few days, for the love he had to her.' There the unscrupulous craft of Laban entrapped him into the false marriage with Leah; but never did Jacob forget that Rachel was his true affianced bride; and his great and faithful love for her lay at the root of all the story of his life.

Thus we read the otherwise difficult riddle: 'these are the generations of Jacob: *Joseph*, seventeen years old,' &c. Padan-Aram was an old home of the fathers of Bible history, and their names still bloom from the soil in the local names Seruj, Kheber-Keui, and the like. Their way of life was not that of mere roving shepherds and herdsmen. Rather its fashion may be found in the Book of Job, who was one of the princes 'sitting in the gate' of the city; whose sons dwelt within 'the four corners of the house,' while they or their shepherds drove afield their wealth of herds with 'the dogs of their flock,' their sons and daughters following this pastoral life, but not forsaking the town, as the Arabs do in these days.

Kharran was a great outpost of the lordship and civilization of Chaldæa, and indeed remained a stronghold of planetary worship for centuries of Christian history, while the neighbouring city Edessa (Urfah) had its church and bishops.

It was in no remote corner of the wilderness that Jacob wooed his well-beloved Rachel, but by the great stream of the world's traffic; where the armies and caravans have beaten their dusty course through all the ages. Cuneiform inscriptions, as well as Fathers of the Church, have told us much of Kharran, and it is likely that antiquarian explorers may yet find in its great mound relics of no slight interest. Elsewhere I have described the place at some length[1]. Here I will only add that it was the very place for that paradoxical

---

[1] *Studies on the Times of Abraham.*

mixture of patriarchal faith, with magical divination and half-idolatrous regard for *teráphim*, which so puzzled the souls of Laban and of Rachel, and which led to the very edge of a frightful tragedy in the camp of the fugitive Jacob. The coherence of the Biblical narrative with external testimony is to be carefully marked in all that relates to Kharran and Padan-Aram ; to the connexion of the 'strangers and pilgrims' of Canaan with that resting-place of generations around the grave of Terakh, their father, which even Abraham still knew as 'my country,' although he charged his trusty Eliezer with most ample reason, 'Beware that thou bring not my son thither again.'

In truth we might well pursue this line of inquiry further. There was no choice except between the 'daughters of Kheth' and other maidens of Canaan on the one hand, and the 'kindred' from Padan-Aram on the other. But many a 'root of bitterness' grew in the fields of Kharran, and as we go on the path of our story we shall often taste the bitter in the wayside cup, and remember whence it came.

So much the more do we bless the 'sweetness and light' of Abraham's faith and walk with God, and rejoice to see Jacob struggling out of the tangled web, albeit sore bested in the 'few and evil' days of the years of his pilgrimage.

Thus, for instance, how pitifully was Jacob withholden from his heart's desire! The son of a wealthy father, the inheritor of the birthright, with his staff alone (the symbol of his dignity) he passed over Jordan. Seven years of drudgery, in heat by day, and frost of wakeful nights, he had to fulfil in payment of the dower of

Rachel; and only to fall into the snare of a double wedlock.

Then came the seven years' further bondage to the crafty and oppressive Laban, years of sorrow and rebuke to the childless Rachel, while she saw the children of the other tents sporting around her, or carried in the arms of their mothers. Thus it seems that Leah had borne Reuben, Simeon, Levi, Judah, and afterwards Issachar and Zebulun, and Dinah her daughter. And Bilhah had become the mother of Dan and Naphtali, and Zilpah of Gad and Asher[1]. But at last, when twice seven years of Jacob's sore service were drawing to an end, 'God remembered Rachel,' and 'she bare a son,' and said, 'God *hath taken away* my reproach,' and she called his name Joseph, and said, 'The Lord *shall add* to me another son.'

Well might the birth of Joseph be a crown of joy to Jacob and Rachel, for their desire was granted. The real destined wife had borne the heir of their hope. And now Jacob would go to his father's house in Canaan a happy man. 'When Rachel had borne Joseph . . . . Jacob said unto Laban, Send me away, that I may go unto mine own place, and to my country.'

For his heart was yearning to meet his father and mother again at 'Kiriath-Arba, which is Hebron,' where Abraham and Isaac sojourned; and Rachel, now that the Lord had taken away her reproach, would 'bring her babe, and make her boast' in the south land, where Isaac had been born in like manner after long years of 'hope deferred.'

It was Rachel who had been brought to Jacob (as

---

[1] Lange, Gen. xxix.

his mother to Eliezer) at the well. She it was for whose sake the seven years had seemed so short. In all piety and righteousness, her first-born was the destined heir; and all along Jacob behaved himself as the constant and loving husband of Rachel, and the faithful father of her children. Let justice be done in this matter, for Jacob has faults enough to answer for. I contend that doting weakness in his dealings with Joseph was not among the number of those frailties. And let us remember that the whole story of Joseph unfolds itself like a flower from this stem of his father's loving preference, which I believe to be a strong point, and not a foible, in the character of Jacob. But the crafty Laban prevailed once more to hold in his toils the man for whose sake he had 'divined' that Jehovah had blessed him, just as the house of Joseph's master was afterwards made to prosper for his sake.

So the first six years of the life of little Joseph were passed in Padan-Aram during the strife of wits between his father and his grandfather; certainly a trying time for all the house, and far less favourable to all that was good, faithful, and noble, than those six years would have been if spent in the Vale of Hebron and the broad pastures of Beer-sheba.

But Jacob was a thriving man, and Laban's sons were envious, and stirred up jealousy in their father. And the God of his fathers bade Jacob begone, for He would be with him. So Jacob 'sent and called *Rachel and Leah* to the field unto his flock,' and set the state of things before them, and they all agreed to flee away; and so fled while Laban was gone to shear his sheep.

Then Joseph saw the great river Euphrates, and was

ferried over, perhaps at Karkemish; and so by Aleppo, and Hamah, and Damascus, they sped as they could on their way to the highlands of Gilead, in the old track trodden by their fathers; and here, after seven days' journey, Laban overtook them, having set out on the third day after Jacob's flight, which, therefore, had been on the tenth day before. And now, in the stormy scene of mutual reproaches, Joseph, the six years' child, may have witnessed in his mother's tent the danger to her life as she sat above the hidden *teráphim*. Little, perhaps, did he understand these unhappy doings on the heights of Gilead. How gladly must he have seen the cairn heaped up, and the upright stone set firmly to bear witness of the covenant at Mizpah!

'And Jacob went on his way, and the angels of God met him: and when Jacob saw them, he said, This is God's host (or camp, *makhaneh*), and he called the name of that place Makhanaïm' (two camps); for there the camp of Jacob was by the camp of the angels. From this place, bright with the presence of God's messengers, Jacob sends his own to Esau, his brother, unto the land of Se'ir; and they return with the alarming report that Esau was coming with four hundred men. Then, with the ingenuity of fear, Jacob divides his whole caravan into two separate companies (the word is *makhaneh*), and prays a thankful, humble, earnest prayer to the God of his fathers to deliver him In the morning he orders his gifts to propitiate Esau in the degrees of dignity; goats, sheep, camels, kine, asses; and puts a space between the droves, and gives a ceremonial message to the leaders, and sends the presents on across the Yabbok (the Zerka of these days), while he stayed in the camp. But in the night he arose, and made to pass across the ford all that was dear to him ; and doubtless Rachel with her child last. And then he was left alone, and One greater than the angels met him. and wrestled with him, and blessed him in the rising of the dawn. And the place Penu-el ('the face of God'), and perhaps the ford and stream Yabbok (as if *the wrestler*), took their names from that great night.

In the life of Jacob, and therefore of Joseph, after the hot strife of craft and jealousy, how freely do we breathe again in these sublime meetings of heaven and earth ! If Joseph in his after-life saw fit, with kind ends in view, to practise ingenious devices after the old style of keen invention, it was from those glorious traditions of his childhood that he learned to witness the good confession : 'so now it was not you that brought me hither, but God.'

Let us divine the feelings of that day, when the long caravan, group after group, passed on to meet the injured and terrible Esau with his four hundred men in arms. First Jacob himself, to bear the earliest brunt, then the handmaids and their boys, then Leah and her children, 'and after came Joseph near and Rachel, and they bowed themselves.' Thus 'Joseph and Rachel' were duly put in the place of greatest safety and dignity.

All was peace. ' So Esau returned that day on his way to Se'ir; and Jacob journeyed to Sukkôth, and built him an house (*bêth*), and made booths (*sukkôth*) for his cattle, therefore the name of the place is called Sukkoth.'

Dr. Merrill has identified this place with Tell Dar'ala [1], just north of the Yabbok, on the strength of a passage in the Talmud which gives the name Der'alah as that of the ancient Sukkôth. Major Conder supports this identification.

[1] *East of Jordan*, p. 385.

CHAPTER II.

SHEKEM.

STILL on the east of Jordan, as it seems, where he had built the house and booths of Sukkôth, Jacob must have lingered a long time before crossing the river. But at length he brought all his train through the turbid stream, probably at the Dâmieh ford; and leading them up the green and watered valley of Fâr'aa, halted at 'Shalem, a city of Shekem.' 'The plain of Mukhna,' says Dr. Porter, 'sends out a broad green arm among the hills on the east, opposite the vale of Nâbulus. The arm is called Sâlim, and takes its name from a little village on the rocky acclivity to the north, doubtless occupying the site, as it retains the name, of "Shalem, a city of Shekem," near which Jacob pitched his tent on his return from Padan-Aram [1].'

Now, since 'the arm' of the Mukhna plain bears the name of Sâlim, and not merely the modern village, this may the better help us to understand how the 'piece of the field where he had spread his tent' should include

---

[1] *Syria and Palestine*, p. 333.

B 2

Jacob's Well and the tomb of Joseph, both of them about two miles and a half westward of Sâlim as it now stands, and about a mile and a quarter from Nablûs. Jacob's encampment would lie between Shalem and Shekem in the green plain.

When Rachel and her little son came up the valley, its masters were of the people called 'the Khivvite.' It is generally taken as a merely descriptive name, meaning 'villagers.' However that may be, we find them in possession of the very fairest spot in all the land of Canaan, under their chieftain Khamor[1], and Shechem his son.

Like Abraham, Jacob consecrated his resting-place in the land of Canaan by building an altar, which he called by the motto : El-elohe-Israël (*El*, the God of Isra-el), expressing the affiance to the mighty God who had upheld and rescued and blessed him, and given him his title, Isra-el. We must not think of the eight or ten years spent at Shalem as a time of pastoral seclusion in a green wilderness. The tribe were still on the high-road of the travel and traffic of those days, as at Kharran, and close to the settled towns of the Canaanites.

As Joseph grew up, a lad 'fair of form and fair of countenance,' with the beauty of his mother and his grandmother, like David long afterwards, he must have seen the sights of town and country, and the foreign caravans that drew their long laden trains down to the great and renowned land of the Pharaohs. He must have heard the gossip of the women, the talk and long entertaining stories of the camp-fire, and the life-lore of

[1] See Appendix A.

Abraham, and Isaac, and Jacob, and of their sires on the other side of the great river. And one word lets out much of their manner of life, which is quite supported by the old-world records of Chaldæa, the very numerous 'contract-tablets' of our museums, and the like; where the men of Semitic and even Hebrew names are constantly found engaging in sales and barter, whether of commodities, or properties, or slaves. For we are told that the sagacious lords of Shekem said to their citizens about the new-comers : ' Let them dwell in the land and trade therein.' It was not merely and altogether the nomadic and pastoral life that we have pictured so familiarly to ourselves. Jacob provided his portion of land with that which made it as much as possible a place of separate and independent life for his own people,—the memorable well, 'deeper far,' says Canon Tristram, 'than the wells sunk by his grandfather Abraham under similar circumstances at Beersheba, and which also remain to this day. We know not the original depth of this well, but it measured some few years ago 105 feet; and probably this falls far short of its original depth, since rubbish has been continually and wantonly thrown in, till it is now choked at a depth of 75 feet[1].'

Mr. Mill states that it is a rain-water cistern, and not a well of living water. This agrees with the contrast in our Saviour's words to the woman of Sychar : ' He would have given thee living water.' Major Conder says that the well is cut through alluvial soil and soft rock, receiving water by infiltration through the sides. ' There

---

[1] For a further account of Jacob's Well, we may refer to the *Memoirs* (vol. ii. p. 172) of the Palestine Survey.

appears to be occasionally as much as two fathoms of water, but in summer the well is dry.'

'By digging this well,' as Major Conder justly observes, 'Jacob avoided those quarrels from which his father had suffered in the Philistine country, pursuing a policy of peace, which appears generally to have distinguished his actions.'

I think we may add another thought. The well's mouth, or the gushing spring of living water, is the great scene of the gathering of women, and Jacob may well have wished to guard those of his own tribe from mingling with 'the daughters of the land.' It was this very thing which, after years of peaceable and prosperous intercourse with the Canaanite town-dwellers, brought about the disgraceful and horrible events so honestly recorded in the family annals. It seems to my mind, in meditating on the life of Joseph, that this 'tale whose lightest word . . . would freeze his young blood' must have been an unforgotten thing in the heart of this noble lad, who was of age to receive its dreadful lessons, and lay up the strong principles of conduct that by God's grace guarded him in the day of trial in the house of Potiphar in Egypt.

The suppressed feelings of the father, which burned forth in his last days, were divined and shared by this beloved son of his old age, and the chastened Israel lived to rejoice that his Rachel's first-born was not a Reuben or a Judah, a Simeon or a Levi.

The whole matter of Dinah, the outrage and the treacherous and villainous plot, the vengeance and the plunder, which broke up all their peace, and made them an abhorrence to the people of the land, must surely have been of vast consequence in building up the character of Joseph. Yet I think it has never received the attention it deserves in this regard.

Little wonder is it that after such things : ' God said unto Jacob, Arise, go up to *Beth-el*, and dwell there : and make thee there an altar unto God (*El*), that appeared unto thee when thou fleddest from the face of Esau thy brother.' Evil were the days that had brought forth such a tale as Jacob had to tell to his father after nearly thirty years. But now he was learning to lean on his young Joseph. With his staff had he passed over Jordan, but now he was returning with Joseph for his staff, the support of his declining years, and the destined star and sceptre of his house.

After the complete sack of the city, there must have been in the hands of the Israelites a large amount of wealth of the kinds most prized—gold, and silver, and garments ; and much of this spoil would have come from the sanctuaries of the gods ; nay, the very gods of the aliens were in their possession, and ornaments of an idolatrous design were in their ears. Although we know that Rachel had hidden and kept her father's *teráphim*, yet we must not hastily suppose that there was extensive idolatry among her people, or in the camp of Jacob. But after the plunder of the city so murderously taken, ' all their little ones and their wives ' were in the hands of Israel as captives, with all that belonged to them ; and these would be especially intended in the expression ' all that were with Jacob,' as distinguished from ' his household.' Therefore it must have been a great and stern transaction when they purified themselves at Jacob's command, and changed their

garments; and he buried all the gods and the earrings
under the oak by Shekem, which seems to be marked
by the name of the present village of Balâta (equivalent
to Ballut, 'an oak'), close to Jacob's Well, if Major Conder
is right.

Doubtless there was the most serious reason to
suppose that the Khivvites, the Canaanites, and the
Perizzites would 'pursue after' these treacherous and
sanguinary sons of Israel. But the 'terror of God'
was upon them, and the march to the old memorable
halting-place of Beth-el was safely accomplished,—a
distance of only about five-and-twenty miles,—by Jacob
'and all the people that were with him;' among them
all the widows and orphans bewailing their dead.

If we would really understand in what fashion the
young man Joseph grew up, we must honestly picture
to ourselves these heart-rending scenes, and the conduct
of the various actors in them. It seems that Rebekah
was dead before this time, but Debôrah, her faithful
nurse, who had been sent away from Kharran with
her and the trusty Eliezer, amidst the benedictions of
her clan so long before, was with the women of the
tribe; and we do not wonder to read that after all
these things, and such a migration, she 'died; and she
was buried beneath Beth-el under an oak; and the
name of it was called The Oak of Weeping.'

Well may they have bewailed this good and faithful
servant of the old times; but we may be sure that
not all the weeping was for her. No hired mourners
were needed at the Oak of Weeping. One would think
that even Simeon and Levi would weep there among
the victims of their wrath—'all the little ones, and

the wives' whom their sword had made widows. Did not young Joseph feel with his father there, ' O my soul, come not into their secret ; unto their assembly, mine honour, be not thou united ! '

This must have been 'a sore mourning' for Jacob, on his return after some thirty years to ' the gate of heaven,' where he had seen

> ' the great world's altar stairs
> That slope through darkness up to God.'

But he was not left unblessed, for 'God appeared unto Jacob again,' and renewed the covenant, and gave the vast word of promise, and ' went up from him,' and left him at ' the gate of heaven ' once more [1].

Doubtless the sights and scenery around him drew Jacob once more to hallowed thoughts and higher conversance. 'Like as a father pitieth his own children,' God had dealt with Israel, in thus visiting him and blessing him after these sore miseries. But the heaviest sorrow of all was close at hand. For the next, and unexpected, halt of this heavy journey was for Joseph's mother to bear her second son, ' as her soul was in departing (for she died).' Was it not the cruel wrath

---

[1] It is not, perhaps, out of place here to say a word as to that celestial vision of Jacob which had won for Beth-el its name. It seems to me that what Jacob saw, reaching from earth to heaven, was not a ladder, but the grand flight of steps which rose so beautifully by successive stages from the wide green levels of Chaldæa to the topmost golden shrine and dwelling of the god.

And the expression ' gate of heaven ' seems to associate itself with another word for gate, which in Chaldæa was applied to sanctuaries, as in Bab-ili, gate of El, and the like.

If these suggestions are just, they will have some bearing on the traditional associations of the ' Syrian ' ('*Arami* '), which came with his fathers from Babylonia.

of Leah's sons that cost the life of Rachel? Jacob
was with her in this saddest day of all his evil days,
and buried her 'by the way to Ephrath, which is
Bethlehem.' The Vulgate (I know not on what textual
authority) tells us 'it was springtide'—('eratque vernum
tempus'). This is so sweet a 'touch of Nature' that it
must surely be a true memory that has floated down
the ages.

There seems no good ground to doubt the correctness
of the old tradition which marks the well-known tomb
of Rachel, not a mile north of Bethlehem. The true
boundary line of Benjamin passes by and goes farther
south, and thus 'agrees with the identical notice [1] of
Rachel's Tomb, which was near Bethlehem, as being on
the border of Benjamin [2].'

The Ramah, where Jeremiah beautifully imagines
Rachel bewailing her children taken captive and slain,
'must have been contiguous to Bethlehem, was subject
to the same calamity [in the days of Herod], and being
near Rachel's tomb, the poetic accommodation of Jeremiah by St. Matthew was natural and beautiful.' Thus
writes Dr. Thomson [3], remarking that it is not strange
that so common a name should have perished, since
any place seated on a hill may be called Ram,
Ramah, &c. ('height').

Jacob's well-beloved wife, for whose sake the long
seven years of servitude had seemed but a few days,
was, as Josephus says, not honoured with a burial at
Hebron; but to this day Jew, Moslem, and Christian
alike respect the place of the pillar set up by Jacob

---

[1] Sam. x. 2.   [2] Conder, *Bible Handbook*, p. 258.
                 [3] *The Land and the Book*, p. 645.

in memory of his great heart-sorrow, ' in the way, when yet there was but a little way to come unto Ephrath.' It is very curious and touching that, by a misappre- hension of a Hebrew word, the place was called by pilgrims long afterwards Chabratha, ' a little way.'

Dean Stanley tells us[1], quoting Schwarz, that there is a cave underneath the tomb of Rachel. This makes it the more likely that it is the true spot ; which, indeed, there is no manner of reason to doubt.

And now the soul of the loving wife and mother had departed, and the ancient nurse of Rebekah was dead, and the babe, son of the mother's anguish (Ben-oni), but son of the father's right hand (Ben-jamin), was left to be brought up with Joseph, then, it seems, about sixteen years old ; and to the tent of Isaac they went, at the old head-quarters of Abraham by Hebron.

Yet one halting-place remained on the way, at Migdol- eder. And there the unutterable outrage fell on Jacob at the hands of his first-born Reuben. Vainly, with shuddering and astonishment, does any feeling heart try to fashion out the reality of a life so

'heated hot with burning fears,
And dipt in baths of hissing tears,
And battered with the shocks of doom.'

[1] *Sinai and Palestine*, p. 149.

CHAPTER III.

HEBRON AND DOTHAN.

IT is an ignorant and false estimate of Jacob's character that would set him down as a man of dull moral perception, and drifted by shallow tides of motive. The very silent intensity of his feelings drove him to ripen them into that fulness of utterance, when 'at the last he spake with his tongue,' which gives a monumental grandeur to the blessings and blame of the departing patriarch.

Under the shadow of these heavy-laden boughs of his father's autumnal life, the young ingenuous Joseph was putting forth the strong shoots of his rising manhood.

At last the heart-weary pilgrim and sojourner filled up the circle of his thirty years' wandering; 'and Jacob came unto Isaac his father unto Mamre unto the city of Arba, which is Hebron, where Abraham and Isaac sojourned.'

This ancient head-quarters of the sons of Anak might well tempt us to linger, and we shall have something to say about its sacred fastness and venerated 'possession of a burying-place,' where Abraham and Sarah were lying in peace at the time when their grandson, heir with them of the covenant of promise, came back laden with his sad wealth of experience, bringing his lost Rachel's first-born Joseph, and the new-born 'son of his right hand,'—all that remained of her under the light of the sun.

'And Jacob dwelt (or remained) in the land of the sojournings of his father, in the land of Canaan.'

Then follows in the Pentateuch one of those important titles or headings of 'generations' (*toledôth*),— a word so hard to do into English. But it is a sequel perfectly in keeping with the whole drift and purpose of Jacob's life that its current should now run in the channel of Joseph's destiny. How obvious and customary would it be if we read : 'These are the generations of Joseph,' when the lad's story was to open before us. But there is, to my mind, a depth of true meaning in the unique form of expression : 'These are the generations (this is the life-story) of Jacob : Joseph, seventeen years old, was feeding the flock with his brethren ;'—and so Jacob's life thenceforth is Joseph's. This is none the less so because we find on the disappearance of Joseph the wretched narrative of the doings of Judah.

We have seen Rachel and Joseph put in the place of honour and of safety throughout our story, and rightly so distinguished. For Rachel was the true destined bride whom Jacob loved and won, *tenax propositi*, with a noble constancy and fortitude, and accordingly we find him emphatically calling her 'my

wife' in speaking of her sons to their brethren [1] ; and
so also is Rachel alone named in the pedigree in the
forty-sixth chapter of Genesis, 'Jacob's wife.' This
deliberate and unswerving preference seems to me the
forte, and not the foible, of Jacob's character, and it
is the very proof of the right temper of the blade,
slight and thin though it may be beside the trusty
strength of Abraham.

Now Rachel was gone, and could no longer uphold
her lad ; and the mother's heart was in Jacob, who
righteously stood fast to Rachel's first-born son. Yet
he let him go 'with the sons of Bilhah,' Dan and
Naphtali, 'and with the sons of Zilpah,' Gad and
Asher ; and he was a lad, probably in the sense of a
serving-lad, with them, as the good and learned old
commentator, Ainsworth, says so sensibly, '*a lad* or
yong man, which word is used not onely for yong in
yeeres, but often for a *servant* or *minister*,—see Gen.
xiv. 24. In this sense it noteth Joseph's humility ; and
how his father, though he loved him most, yet brought
him up without idlenesse or cockering.'

It was not from any such motive as 'cockering' that
Jacob clad his chosen son in the garment of honour
which figures so brightly in our imagination. Much
learned controversy has thrown its dust upon the 'coat
of many colours.' But I believe that its first beauty
remains fresh after all. Whether, indeed, as Professor
Blunt supposed [2], it may have been a sacerdotal garment
in particular, we may doubt ; although the dignity of
the birthright involved the patriarchal priesthood, and it

[1] Gen. xliv. 27.
[2] *Undesigned Coincidences*, p. 16.

was as consecrated from among his brethren ('separated')[1] that he wore this goodly garment, as we may well suppose. As to its appearance, I think, after a good deal of inquiry and consideration, that the Septuagint (χιτῶνα ποικίλον) and the Vulgate (*tunicam polymitam*), both of which convey the idea of a variegated tunic, a veritable 'coat of many colours,' are right; and that the *passim* of the Hebrew were pieces or 'patches' of bright colours, used in the ornamental *appliqué* work still so much in fashion in Eastern countries.

The Egyptian pictures show us that from a time long before that of Abraham the Semitic nations of Western Asia wore coats and kilts of very richly coloured designs, in white, blue, red, green, and other colours, and that the chieftain was distinguished by the especial form and ornamentation of his tunic. The celebrated procession of the Amu (Asiatic foreigners) on the wall of a subterranean tomb at Beni-Hassan, figured by Champollion, Rosellini, and Lepsius in their magnificent works, and reproduced in colours by Dr. Birch in his edition of Wilkinson's *Ancient Egyptians*[2], is the earliest example, and perhaps the best.

We are the more inclined to be sure on this matter from the same word in effect (*pesh*) in Egyptian, as a verb signifying 'to *divide* in two parts,' and the Coptic *pôsh*, meaning 'division'[3], &c. It is thus *patch-work*.

We are told that 'Israel loved Joseph more than all his children, because he was the son of his old age.' The expression is only used besides with reference to Isaac and to Benjamin[4], and Jewish com-

---

[1] Gen. xlix. 26.
[2] Vol. i. p. 180.
[3] Pierret, *Vocabulaire*, pp. 157, 158.
[4] Gen. xxi. 2, 7; xliv. 20.

mentators have taken it as expressing the position of usefulness and duty occupied by that son who remained at home with his father as the help and staff of his old age [1]. And doubtless such a post was really filled by Isaac towards Abraham, and by Joseph, and afterwards by Benjamin, towards their father Jacob. But it is spoken of Isaac at his very birth.

It could not be but that Joseph walked in paths of danger among those unruly brethren, sons of different mothers ; but none of them born of his own, the beloved and lost Rachel. When we remember the outrage of Reuben, so recent as it was, the fearful vindictive cruelty of Simeon and Levi, and the ill-regulated life of Judah, it is easy to conjecture the difficulties and pitfalls that beset the life of Joseph, who on the one hand had to serve his brethren in the affairs of daily life, and on the other was bound above all to be loyal, open-hearted, and faithful to their father.

Archdeacon Norris writes with truth : ' The memory of his mother, the charge of that motherless child whom he loved with more than a brother's love, and above all the influence of his father ever growing in spirituality—all this served to keep Joseph pure amid the evil examples of his elder brothers.'

The ingenuous lad told his father of their ill-doing : and they envied and hated him, and could not even salute him with the ordinary courtesy of life. But he had not the shrewdness to suppress in their company things that would be sure to rouse their ill-will to a still greater height.

Portentous dreams were regarded as very important

[1] Lange on Gen. xxxvii. 3.

omens, and Joseph told his brethren of a dream whose meaning was plain enough. In this dream the mixture of the agricultural with the pastoral life was clearly shown ; and in this regard it forms important material for our estimate of the way of life of those patriarchal families. In the expression, ' my sheaf arose, and also stood upright, and, behold, your sheaves stood round about and bowed down to my sheaf,' we are reminded of the harvest scenes in Egyptian pictures, where the sheaves are not set upright, as with us, but laid flat on their sides on the ground. In this dream the scene of Joseph's future supremacy, the long harvest plain of Egypt, was fore-shadowed.

The next portended a still greater exaltation, in which ' the sun and moon ' stood for his father and mother ; and ' eleven stars ' (not ' *the* eleven stars,' as in our Authorised Version) were his eleven brethren. Although the suggestion of the signs of the Zodiac is unfounded, it does not follow that the series of twelve which Joseph's own star would have completed did not refer to some familiar system. Such sets of twelve stars were well-known at that time, as we may read in Lenormant's learned work, *Les Origines de l'Histoire* [1]. But I think the most likely system of twelve may be found in Professor Sayce's important paper [2] on Early Babylonian Astronomy, where we read of ' the twelve stars of Martu, or the West,' whose names he recites, including Jupiter, Mercury (the planet which was ' the lord of the men of Kharran,' Joseph's own birth-place), and Mars, with nine fixed stars.

[1] Vol. i. pp. 501, 591.
[2] *Trans. Soc. Bib. Arch.* iii. p. 176.

This second dream Joseph told to his father, who was involved in it as well as his brethren : 'and his father rebuked him, and said unto him, What is this dream that thou hast dreamed ? Shall I and thy mother and thy brethren indeed come to bow down ourselves to thee to the earth ?' The eleven stars clearly show that Benjamin was already left in Rachel's void place ; but then how could his mother shine upon her Joseph in this strange dream ? Jacob kept it in his heart, with many an unspoken thing beside. And this was the turning-point in Joseph's life. His brethren were bold enough to go back with the flock to the scene of their evil exploits'; and Jacob's heart misgave him as to their peace, and the peace of the flock ; and, at his father's bidding, the son of his home set forth to inquire of their welfare, like David so long after.

A man found him 'wandering in the field' at Shekem, and doubtless his thoughts were wandering too, for this was the scene of his harvest-dream, no less than of the dreadful and the tender thoughts of father, mother, sister, brethren. Very easily might Joseph have excused himself for returning to his father at Hebron. But the man told him where to find his brethren, and the brave lad went on to Dothan. He had drunk of Jacob's Well for the last time.

The distance he traversed was more than fifteen English miles before Joseph found his brethren, as he had been told, at Dothan, which still keeps its old name, Tell Dothan. This place was an important halting-place on the great caravan-road from Damascus into Egypt, and we find the name (Duthina) inscribed not very long afterwards in the Karnak Lists of Thothmes III. This identification was first proposed by the late learned Rev. D. H. Haigh[1] in 1875, and is generally accepted. 'Dothan,' writes Canon Tristram, 'is the very richest of pasture-grounds—a little upland plain, with a smooth hill, at the southern end of which are some ruins, and a fine spring bursting out at its foot.'

Major Conder mentions two wells very near together, and in fact there are many cisterns of this kind, contracted towards the top in the shape of a bottle, and for the most part dry even in the winter. One in particular gives its name to the khan close by, 'the Khan of Joseph's Pit.' The place was a very orchard of lemons, oranges, and pomegranates not many years since, as we are told by the Abbé Vigouroux in his learned and valuable work, *La Bible et les Découvertes Modernes*[2].

Here it was then that the brethren of Joseph saw their young brother drawing near to them, easily recognized by his handsome tunic. But while he was yet far off they took counsel together to kill the 'master of dreams,' and throw him into one of the deep wells; and say, 'A wild beast has eaten him,' and see what would become of his dreams. We know the story. They saw the anguish of his soul, but would not hear. Reuben saved his life by persuading them not to kill him first, but simply to throw him into an empty pit, intending to draw him out and take him to their father. And they did it, and Reuben left them; but when he returned there was no Joseph. They had sold him to Ishmaelite traders from the land of Midian, going down from Gilead into Egypt. This was Judah's doing, and

---

[1] *Zeitschr. f. Aeg. Spr.* p. 101. [2] Vol. ii. p. 9.

once more the noble lad's life was saved on that day. But the Ishmaelites paid their twenty pieces of silver (a cheap bargain), and took their goodly slave among their other merchandise, and went their way up the gradual ascent, by the road which Joseph had so eagerly traversed on his anxious father's errand.

It is easy to ascertain that spices must have formed a most important part of the traffic with Egypt, where enormous quantities were needed for compounding the incense of the temple-worship, and for embalming the dead. The three kinds of produce mentioned are the same as those afterwards sent by Jacob as a gift to Joseph, namely, the gum of the *Astragalus traga-cantha*, still called *naka'at* by the Arabs, the identical name used in the narrative, *nekōth;* the balm of Gilead, *tsori;* and the *ladanum*, from the *Cistus ladaniferus*, which was introduced into Egypt for cultivation in Ptolemaic times, and before that imported from the East.

Dr. Ebers has found two of these, under the names *nekpat* and *tsara*, among the ingredients of the celebrated incense Kyphi in an Egyptian papyrus[1]. These precious things were brought from the Lebanon and Gilead, and the spices of Canaan and of Syria are repeatedly mentioned in general terms in the papyri of Egypt. But however valuable these gums and aromatics were in the eyes of the Ishmaelites of Midian, it is certain that slaves were still more coveted; and male and female slaves from *Khal*, or Syria, were most highly esteemed, and, as Brugsch writes, 'were procured by

Aegypten, &c. p. 290.

distinguished Egyptians at a high price, whether for
their own houses or for service in the holy dwellings of
the Egyptian gods[1].'

There is something in the gradation of value among
slaves in Egypt which especially affects the life of Joseph
in more ways than one. He was, like his mother Rachel,
and Sarah before her, fair of countenance, and the same
beauty of complexion which brought Sarah into so great
peril would make Joseph the more esteemed as a slave.
Dr. Ebers writes on this subject with regard to the
Egyptians: 'Their complexion itself had become
darkened through climatic influence and obscuration of
the blood by admixture of race with blacks, for on the
one hand we see, even on the oldest monuments, the men
and women of rank painted more fair than the ordinary
man; on the other hand, the word *ami*, the fair-com-
plexioned, stands distinctly for "belonging to a higher
class," and, taken in opposition to *hon* and *hon-t* (male
and female slave), used for "free man" in the sentence :
"fair people 5, slaves and female slaves with their
children 1579[2]." It seems likely that the fair and goodly
Joseph would not be regarded as an ignoble captive, but
as high and well-born, when "stolen out of the land of
the Hebrews."'

In the anguish of his soul, Joseph was carried away past
his father's green valley and deep well, past his mother's
grave, past the very home at Hebron, on the distant
height, where Jacob had so lately bid him farewell on his
brotherly errand. If he even saw them now, it was for
the last time. But it is perhaps more likely that the
Ishmaelites wrapped him up on the camel, for fear of

[1] *Hist.* vol. i. p. 222.   [2] *Aegypten, &c.* p. 52.

rescue or flight, as Sir Samuel Baker's lad was hurried away hidden in a gum-sack[1].

Meanwhile the cruel and unnatural brethren carry out to the uttermost their scheme. Jacob had used the 'goodly raiment' of Esau and the dainty meat of the kid to deceive his father. His sons bring the coat of Joseph dipped in the blood of a kid to their father, with the cynical challenge: 'Know now whether it be thy son's coat or no.'

Jacob rends his mantle and clothes his loins in sack-cloth, and refuses comfort: 'For I will go down to my son mourning to Sheol.' Of course he did not mean 'into the grave,' as it is unfortunately given in our Authorised Version, but into *Hades*, where he should yet meet his Joseph, whom the wild beast had devoured: while his own wearied body might lie in the Makpelah, or beside Rachel in the wayside of Ephrath.

The misery of Jacob must have been all the more severe, since this 'most foul and most unnatural' act of cruelty must have been committed almost immediately on Jacob's coming to Hebron, as Dean Alford has shown in a note[2] to this effect. Isaac's age was sixty at Jacob's birth[3]. Jacob was one hundred and twenty years old at Isaac's death, and one hundred and thirty at the migration to Egypt[4], when Joseph was between thirty-nine and forty[5]. But, as Joseph was seventeen when sold, and Jacob's migration was twenty-three years later, Isaac must have survived Joseph's sale between twelve

---

[1] Vigouroux, *La Bible*, &c. vol. ii. p. 20.
[2] *Genesis*, p. 158.
[3] Gen. xxv. 26.   [4] Gen. xlvii. 9.
[5] Cf. Gen. xli. 46, 47, and xlv. 6.

and thirteen years, until the time of his grandson's exaltation in Egypt. Hence also Joseph was sold immediately on Jacob's coming to Hebron. And how soon after his mother's death[1]!

[1] Delitzsch, *New Commentary*, Gen., vol. ii. pp. 219, 237, 265.

CHAPTER IV.

THERE seems more and more reason to hold the ancient belief that Joseph entered and ruled Egypt during the domination of the Hyksôs, or Shepherd-kings. The best historians of Egypt support this conclusion, as Birch, Brugsch, Maspero, Wiedemann. Eusebius (about A.D. 300) gives the tradition, and George the Syncellus (about A.D. 800) specifies Aphōphis as the Pharaoh of Joseph. The name is an authentic record of the title of two, at all events, of the Hyksôs kings, both in Manetho's lists and on the monuments.

The name Apepi is inscribed on the right shoulder of the grim and striking sphinxes found among the ruins of Sân (Zoan). It is true that Professor Maspero considers this as an usurpation of an older statue. But Mr. Flinders Petrie still believes that the stern features which look out of those shaggy lions' manes are really those of the Shepherd-king. Moreover, in his last and highly important excavations among the ruins of Bubastis (the Pibeseth of Scripture and Tel-Basta of

the present day), M. Naville has recovered twin statues
in fragments, which he believes to be those of a later
Apepi (probably of Joseph's time). The head and other
portions of one of these are now in the British Museum,
and we will say more of them by and by.

There is a very attractive mystery in the origin and
doings of these alien dynasties who ruled Egypt during
some centuries, and are known to us under the general
name of Shepherd-kings. From very early times the
delta of the Nile had been, like the country at the head
of the Persian Gulf, occupied by a mixed population, and
liable to great changes and dangers of invasion. At last,
after the thirteenth Egyptian dynasty of Pharaohs, a
real victory was achieved by foreign lords, who became
Kings of Lower Egypt and over-lords of the Upper Valley
of the Nile for five centuries, as it is generally believed.
As in other cases of conquest by hordes driven on from
without, the questions of race are complicated. It does
not follow from the ethnic affinities of the great mass of
incursive population that the leaders are of the same
race. Rather than this it is often true that they belong
to some superior pedigree, and wield the physical forces
of turbulent clans, who gladly follow the more sagacious
and successful leaders.

After all the sifting of this question it is becoming
more and more credible that the high-road of this great
migration led across the Euphrates from the East to
Northern Syria, and so through Palestine, and that some
strong impulses setting in from beyond the Tigris (as
in the case of Kedorla'omer and kindred over-lords
from Elam) drove on the great migratory hordes with
wives and children, herds and horses, in the same

fashion as the Libyan tribes of the West fell on Lower Egypt in the days of Merenptah, and afterwards in the reign of Rameses III.

It is an interesting thing that the title Salatis, given for the earliest Hyksôs ruler, is the Chaldæan *shallit*, and that in Gen. xlii. 6, Joseph, Viceroy of a Hyksôs Apepi, is called *hash-shallit*, the ruler. Moreover, it is also curious that (as Lenormant has noticed) many centuries later the Assyrians gave the Pharaoh, besides that title, the appellation *Shiltannu* (sultan), which they did not apply to any other sovereign[1].

It must have been towards the close of the long rule of the Shepherd-kings that the lad Joseph, seventeen years of age, was brought down in the long caravan of the Midianites through the fortified frontier of Eastern Egypt and sold into slavery to Potiphar, who is twice noted in the narrative as 'an Egyptian' in Egypt, which is very natural when the sovereign and those of his race were foreign conquerors. Here he was, although under bondage, in very high service in the retinue of a chief officer of the court. Syrian slaves were greatly valued, and especially those well-born and highly educated, and apt for intelligent service.

Potiphar appears to have commanded the body-guard of the Pharaoh. His name is purely Egyptian. Dr. Malan resolves it as Pet-p-har, 'given by Horus.' Potiphera is Pet-p-râ (the gift of Râ, the sun-god), and it is curious to find in a papyrus of the Louvre both the gods combined in the name Peti-hor-p'ra[2].

Joseph, deservedly trusted, falls under the fierce resent-

---

[1] *Hist. Anc. de l'Orient*, 9th ed. vol. ii. p. 147.
[2] Deveria, *MSS. Egyptiens*, p. 100.

ment of his master's abandoned wife. It is interesting to find this incident in the Egyptian story of 'The Two Brothers.' Whether it is an echo of the history of Joseph is doubtful. At any rate, we are shown that an Egyptian writer would bring such an episode into a romantic narrative, the celebrated Orbiney papyrus. The position of a trusted slave as *major-domo* in charge of all the household and property was a thoroughly Egyptian institution.

The lord of Joseph throws him into the royal prison, which is here called *beth hassohar*, which Dr. Ebers has explained as an Egyptian expression, *bita sohar*, the house of the citadel, where the chief of the guard, or commandant, would reside. Here he meets with two other prisoners of high position, the chief butler and the chief baker of the Pharaoh. They relate to him the dreams that had troubled their minds, and Joseph explains them. We need not prove the attention paid in Egypt, as in other ancient nations, to dreams and visions of the night.

A tablet on the breast of the great sphinx commemorates a remarkable dream of Thothmes IV. as he lay weary under his shadow; and readers of Egyptian lore will never forget the story of the possessed Princess of Bakhtan. With regard to the dreams themselves, they are thoroughly Egyptian in their scene and circumstances, especially the subsequent dream of Pharaoh himself. The Nile-stream and flood, and the sacred kine, seven in number, belong entirely to the religion of the land; and it has been shown by the late Canon Cook and others, that the very words that are used in the narrative, as also in the Book of Exodus, are constantly Egyptian words.

With regard to the pressing of the grapes into the Pharaoh's cup, which has been difficult to explain, Sir Gardner Wilkinson writes that 'grape juice, or wine of the vineyard (one of the most delicious beverages of a hot climate, and one that is commonly used in Spain, and other countries of the present day), was among the most noted denominations introduced into the list of offerings on the monuments[1].'

The punishment of the chief baker seems to have been decapitation, which was an Egyptian punishment, followed by the hanging of the body on a gibbet, as Amenhotep II. hung the bodies of some slain Kings of Syria on his galley, and afterwards on the walls of a fortress. The dream of the Pharaoh introduces Joseph to his presence, and the circumstance that Joseph shaved himself is again absolutely Egyptian, for Semitic people have ever abhorred this ceremony, which was essential in the eyes of the Egyptians; and we must remember that the Shepherd-kings kept the Egyptian ceremonial at their court. The exaltation of an Asiatic foreigner to be a great officer of State might have taken place at any period under the Pharaohs, but most easily under the Shepherd-kings, as they were themselves Asiatic foreigners. The phrase attributed to the Pha-

---

[1] I would add that the Hebrew word for pressing the grapes is only here used in the whole Bible. It is *shakhat*, in Chaldee שחט, *sakhat*, 'to squeeze out grapes, Gen. xl. 11' (Gesenius). But an Egyptian verb of similar sound, *sekht*, is used to denote the moulding of bricks by pressure of the clay (Pierret, *Vocab.* p. 536). If it be thought that the office of chief baker was not of great importance, it is well to know that the Scribe of the King's Table, 'Chief of the Loaves,' commemorated by a tablet mentioned by M. Chabas, was also First Lieutenant of the King, or Prime Minister. The great Egyptologist just quoted has treated of the various offices mentioned in connection with Joseph in his *Mélanges Egyptologiques*, 3me série, p. 137.

raoh, 'a man in whom the Spirit of God is,' would be as natural in the mouth of an Egyptian as of a Chaldæan, for such expressions are found in very ancient passages of the Ritual.

CHAPTER V.

JOSEPH IN OFFICE.

WE now come to the highly interesting account of the honours bestowed upon Joseph, and the titles of dignity conferred upon him; and here we are thoroughly at home in the Egyptian Court. 'Pharaoh took off the ring from his hand, and put it upon Joseph's hand.' This was the formal delivery of office by the signet or seal-ring. This is called *teb* in Egyptian, in Hebrew טבעת, *finger*-ring. It had a stone, or a flat surface of gold, engraven for sealing. Such Egyptian rings are among the most beautiful jewels in our museums. A most rare and interesting specimen is described in the catalogue of the collection of M. Allemant (Ancien Interprète de S. M. le Sultan Abd-ul-Aziz), exhibited in London in the year 1878: 'No. 705. San-Tanis. Black jasper. Stone of a ring or seal graven in intaglio (*gravé en creux*) on both sides. On the front a winged serpent and two Semitic signs; on the back a Hebrew inscription. Epoch of the Shepherd-kings, XVIIth dynasty. A very curious and rare piece; probably unique.' It is much to be regretted that the signs and inscription are not given. This relic is a most important illustration of Semitic influence in the Delta at the very period of which we are treating. The winged serpent is very suggestive.

A magnificent tablet of an earlier age described by de Rougé commemorates 'Antef, Prime Minister ("First Deputy of the King").' The long eulogy has many points which illustrate the subsequent dignities of Joseph, 'functionary of *the signet* . . . . chief of the chiefs, ... alone in the multitude, he bears *the word* to men; he declares all affairs in the double Egypt; he speaks on all matters in the place of secret counsel. When he enters he is applauded, when he issues forth, he is praised. . . . The princes hold themselves attentive to his mouth . . . . all his words come to pass without (resistance). like that which issues from the mouth of God[1]'. Nothing can be more close to the details of Joseph's honours than such expressions as these. The words in Genesis xli. 40, 'At thy mouth shall all my people kiss,' are very characteristic. Before the Pharaoh a subject would kiss the ground. The ordinary attitude of submissive attention was that of kissing the hand before the master: 'Be seated, thy hand to thy mouth,' as Pierret quotes from a papyrus. But Chabas supposes that the phrase indicates the elevation of Joseph to the dignity mentioned in an inscription of the XVIIIth dynasty by the title which he renders as '*Grande Bouche Superieure dans le pays tout entier.*' We may also compare the title, 'The Mouth of the King of Upper Egypt,' cited by Maspero[2].

---

[1] *Monuments de Louvre,* p. 73.

[2] The title translated 'Father to Pharaoh' (Gen. xlv. 8) represents an

The collar of gold, of different degrees of elaboration and splendour, was worn by all Egyptians of high rank, and bestowed with much ceremony by the sovereign on those whom he delighted to honour. It is called by an Egyptian name *rebid*, in Egyptian *repit*. 'The greatest honour conferred on Joseph,' says Sir G. Wilkinson, 'was permission to ride in the second chariot which he—the king —had. This was a royal chariot, no one being allowed to appear in his own in the presence of majesty, except in battle.'

This brings before us a notable addition to the force and pomp of Egypt since the days of Abraham. The Pharaoh has chariots, and horses are mentioned as belonging not only to the court but to the people. Now, previously to the Hyksôs dynasties, there is no more evidence of horses in the monuments than in the Scriptures ; but in two celebrated inscriptions of the age now in question, in the tombs of El-Kab, we find them mentioned ; and it appears that horses were introduced from the East into Egypt during the rule of the Hyksôs.

M. Naville writes, 'The other day I came across a picture which reminded me strongly of Joseph and his employment[1]. It has been taken from a tomb. There

Egyptian rank ' Ab en Peraa,' the Head of the Court. And the title ' Adōn' is also truly Egyptian, and designates the office of deputy of the Pharaoh (Brugsch, *Rev. Egyptologique*, vol. i. p. 22).

In the Museum at Turin is a very important sepulchral tablet commemorating the rank and virtues of Beka, superintendent of the royal granary, overseer of Upper and Lower Egypt, of the date of the XIXth or XXth dynasty. Chabas, in describing this tablet, remarks that Beka's functions must have included those of Joseph at the court of the Pharaoh (*Trans. S. Bib. Arch.* vol. v. p. 461. *Papyrus Abbott*, p. 7).

[1] It is in Lepsius, *Denkm.* vol. iii. pp. 76, 77, and Prisse, *Monuments*, pl. 39-42.

you see the King Amenophis III. sitting on his throne, and before him one of his ministers, Chaemha, who seems to have had a very high position. He is called the *Chief of the granaries of the whole kingdom.* Behind him are a great number of officials of different classes, bringing the tribute of the whole land. This man seems to have had nobody above him, as he speaks to the king himself; and he had under his command all the tax-gatherers, and all that concerned the granaries. Besides, he has this strange title, *the Eyes of the King in the towns of the South, and his Ears in the Provinces of the North;* which implies that he knew the land perfectly; and that, like Joseph, "he had gone throughout all the land of Egypt[1]". I think Brugsch mentions Chaemha in his history, but I do not remember whether he points to his resemblance with Joseph, which I find particularly striking; considering that Joseph seems to have been a purely civil officer, and to have had nothing to do with the military class, which, however, must have been powerful under Apophis, who had wars during his reign.' When Joseph was conducted in state in the royal chariot through the capital, the cry of the heralds before him was '*Abrek!*' a word which has never yet received a fully-accepted explanation. Chabas says that it is still the cry to the camel to kneel[2]. The word has been compared with the Assyrian *abarakku*, from Akkadian *abrik*, 'seer.' But Brugsch explains it by the Egyptian word *bark*, 'to kneel, to adore[3].' Mr. Lepage Renouf has, however, met with a passage in a hieratic papyrus lately acquired by the British Museum

---

[1] Gen. xli. 46.   [2] *Études*, p. 412.
[3] Pierret, *Vocab.* p. 126.

which appears to contain the expression (*ȧbu-re-k*), which he regards as signifying 'thy commandment is the object of our desire;' 'we are,' in other words, 'at thy service[1].'

This is, I believe, the last proposed explanation of the enigmatic *abrek*. Professor Sayce has, however, kindly furnished me, at my request, with a note on the Assyrian derivation: '*Abrek*,' he writes, 'is the Assyro-Babylonian *abrikku*, which was borrowed from the Akkadian *abrik*, according to a tablet (82.2.18). The word also appears in Assyrian under the form *abarakku*. The name is interpreted "seer" in the lexical tablets. The title would have been given to Joseph in consequence of his interpretation of dreams.'

The Pharaoh gave a new, and doubtless Egyptian, name to his viceroy, which is expressed in Hebrew letters as צפנת פענח. This was in accordance with custom in such cases, but there has been very much conjecture as to the composition of the Egyptian title and its significance. It has been noticed by Mariette and Lenormant that Ka-mes, the Theban king, about contemporary with our Apepi, assumed a title, *Tsaf-en-to*, which means nourisher of the land; and this entirely agrees with the former part of Joseph's new name[2]. The latter part of Joseph's title, פענח, *p-ānkh*, which

---

[1] *Proc. S. Bib. Arch.* 1888, p. 7.

[2] Brugsch, in noticing this, adds in a note: 'Proper names composed with *Sezaf-*, or with *zaf*, are not rare in Egyptian. It is thus that the name of a king of the XIIIth dynasty begins with this word *Sezaf-*, and that two other Pharaohs of the same dynasty are called *Mer-zefau* ('friend of abundance'), and *Neb-zefau* ('master of abundance'). *Histoire d'Egypte*, p. 169. He explains that: 'The country called "the district of the town Aå-ānkh" (literally "town of life") is the same that the Greek geographers designated

literally means *the life*, is capable of several explanations. Brugsch would refer it to a god of an Eastern
nome of the Delta, as we have seen, but Pierret gives the
word as used for a title of the Pharaoh ; and if this were
so at the time in question, the meaning would be very
appropriate to Joseph as 'Nourisher of the land of the
Pharaoh.' I cannot say that the suggestion of Steindorff[1]
commends itself to my mind.

The Pharaoh provides for his high minister as a fitting
wife a lady of very exalted rank, daughter of the high-
priest of On[2]. M. Naville has very well said: ' I believe
that the king did it on purpose to have one of his men
connected with the most ancient and the most venerated
college of priests. The importance of Heliopolis as a
religious centre comes out in many inscriptions, and it is
natural that Apophis should attempt to create a link
between his government and those priests, who most
likely were of pure Egyptian origin. The priests in
general must have been very powerful at that time, when
we see Joseph respecting all their privileges, while he
taxed so heavily the rest of the country[3].'

The name of Joseph's wife אסנת (Asenath) is ex-

---

by the name of the Sethroïtic Nome. It is this country, situated near Tanis,
where Joseph and the Hebrews lived during the time of their sojourn in Egypt.'
It is true that the god Tum is called in inscriptions found by M. Naville at
Pithom, *Nuter aā ankh*, 'the great living god' (*Store-city of Pithom*, pp.
15, 16; pl. vii. A). Dr. Wiedemann is of opinion that ' the most likely Egyptian etymology is Pa-sent-en-pa-Ānkh, "the strengthener of life" (cf. Lepsius, *Chronol.* p. 382)' (*Sammlung Altaegyptischer Wörter, &c.* p. 21).

[1] *Zeitschr. f. Aeg. Spr.* 1889, p. 41.

[2] See Appendix B.

[3] Dr. Kurt Sethe has given an account of the worship, holy places, and
ministry of Râ during the old empire of Egypt in the *Zeitschrift* for 1889,
pp. 111 *et seqq.*, in which the exact hieroglyphic titles of the priests and pro-

plained by Egyptologists as 'belonging to Neith,' the great goddess. Her father is characteristically called 'the gift of Râ,' the sun-god.

To return now to the state of Egypt at the time of Joseph's viceroyalty. The time, as we believe, was drawing towards the close of the domination of the Hyksôs. The reluctant patriots of Egypt kept up and strengthened at Thebes the rival power of native princes, whose most interesting representative, the last of the three kings called Seqenen-Râ, now lies in the flesh in the Egyptian Museum of Gizeh, near Cairo, bearing fearful marks of the wounds by which he died in battle.

There is a celebrated papyrus (sadly mutilated) which tells of the culmination of a long rivalry of religions, the Sutekh-worship of the Hyksôs being put forward in an exclusive way by the last Apepi in an embassy to one of the Seqenen-Râs. It has been debated which of the three successive kings of this name who ruled at Thebes this may have been, but it now seems likely that the third, the 'very valiant,' was the man, and although he is there said to be merely a *haq*, or subordinate ruler, yet in his time he assumed full Pharaonic titles. It is, how-ever, to be remembered that it was some time later than this that the founder of the XVIIIth Egyptian dynasty, Aahmes, succeeded in driving the foreign lords right out of Egypt, and pursuing them into Southern Palestine.

phets of the great sun-god are recorded. That god was worshipped under the symbolism of the obelisk, which had its endowments and hierarchy.

CHAPTER VI.

AGES before this the splendour of Egyptian civilization had been fully developed, and the monuments, especially of the great IVth and XIIth dynasties, bear witness to a refinement and elaboration in the arts of social life which is altogether unequalled elsewhere at those early periods of the world's history.

The regal pomp of the court, the perfect order of administration down to the lowest details, the disciplined subordination of all ranks and offices, the magnificence of art, and the high development of agriculture and horticulture, under the genial climate, and with the fertilizing conditions of the Nile-floods and irrigation, concern us here in estimating the material which Joseph had in his hands.

For the days of despotic violence and destruction were long past, and probably the ordered system of government was as well established and worked as smoothly as that of British India in the present day. Especially we must now regard the culture of the black and fruitful soil of the long green Nile valley, dependent wholly as it is upon the annual rising and overflow of the Nile. The details of farm-work are before our eyes in all their branches.

In our museums we have implements of husbandry, to which Mr. Flinders Petrie has now added most primeval sickles of wood, the cutting edge of which is formed of flint saws. He has also brought home the wooden corn-shovel of a date earlier than Joseph, and the wooden hoes and ploughshares fit for the light soil. The grain was sown broadcast from the hand, and trodden by flocks of sheep into the moistened soil. When ripe for harvest it was reaped high up towards the ear, and not with short stubble as by us. The sheaves were bound and laid flat on the ground. The grain was thrashed out by the treading of oxen, and when winnowed was put into sacks, cleverly made to balance on the shoulder, and then poured into the great granaries through openings in the roof.

All these operations were methodically carried out under the eyes of stewards, and bailiffs, and gangers ; and registered by scribes with that perfection of method so characteristic of the Egyptians, the actual inventors of red tape.

Although it may appear at first sight in the Book of Genesis that *all* the produce of the seven rich years was stored, yet the definite proposal in Gen. xli. 34 to 'fifth the land' must guide us in construing the rest; and, as Archdeacon Norris has shown, it is likely enough that, taking into account the extreme productiveness of the seven plentiful years, Joseph had 'in his granaries enough to sustain the people at the ordinary rate of consumption during seven years of absolute barrenness.' But of course the example would be largely followed, and all would not depend on the government stores. It was not till 'all the land of Egypt was famished' that the people 'cried to Pharaoh for bread.'

M. Naville remarks : 'How very Egyptian verse 49 of the same chapter; compare line 11 of the great tablet of Abu Simbel : "I will give thee corn in abundance, to enrich Egypt in all times; the wheat is like the sand of the shore ; the granaries reach the sky, and the heaps are like mountains." '

Dean Milman remarks on the agrarian law of the Hebrews : 'The outline of this plan may have been Egyptian. The king of that country, during the administration of Joseph, became proprietor of the whole land, and leased it out on a reserved rent of one-fifth, exactly the two-tenths or tithes paid by the Israelites[1].' Mr. Finn writes : 'To this day in Palestine the cultivator gives the owner of the land one-fifth, if he has found not only labour, but cattle and seed. If the owner gives cattle and seed as well, the cultivator only gets one-fifth of the produce[2].'

The Arab historians El-Makrizi and Abd-el-Latif, of the eleventh and twelfth Christian centuries, describe fearful famines in Egypt, the former of which lasted seven years. The details of starvation are full of horror, and are partly given by Dean Stanley.

As regards the famine of Joseph's own time, it has

[1] *History of the Jews*, vol. i. p. 231.

[2] During Syrian rule the Jews ' paid one-third of the produce of all that was sown, and one half of that from fruit-trees' (Edersheim, *Jewish Social Life*, p. 52). On the division of the land in Egypt, see *Revue Egyptologique*, 1883, p. 101.

been noticed that from an earlier age it was the boast of
Egyptian governors that they had so provided for cultivation and storage that there had been no starvation in
their times; or that famines had been relieved by their
providence and energy.

But Brugsch has stated his conviction that an inscription in a tomb at El-Kab refers to the identical famine.
In this inscription the deceased governor, named Baba,
declares that he collected the harvests, and so provided
that when a famine arose lasting many years he issued
corn to the hungry. There is reason to believe that this
Baba, 'about the same time that Joseph exercised his
office, under one of the Hyksôs kings, lived and worked
under the native King Ra-Sekenen Taā III. in the old
town of El-Kab. The only just conclusion is that
the many years of famine in the time of Baba must
precisely correspond with the seven years of famine
under Joseph's Pharaoh, one of the Shepherd-kings[1].'
This Theban king is the same subject and rival of
Apepi of whom I have before spoken. It may be
that the governor of El-Kab acted under the supreme
direction of Joseph, for it is expressly stated in
the papyrus before quoted (*Sallier Papyrus*) that the
whole land brought its productions to Apepi at Avaris
(Hauar), and that Seqenen-Râ was under him as his
suzerain. Thus, the worthy Baba may well have acted
on general directions from the Delta. He says, ' I issued
corn to the city.' Joseph 'laid up the food in the cities,'
and 'as for the people, he removed them to cities, from
(one) end of the borders of Egypt even to the (other)
end thereof.' That is, where the food was stored, thither

---

[1] *Egypt under the Pharaohs,* vol. i. p. 262.

he gathered the people out of the famine-stricken open country.

With regard to the annual overflow of the Nile, Sir Francis de Winton, in his presidential address to the Geographical Section of the British Association at Newcastle, has given his opinion in view of Mr. Stanley's intelligence of the desiccation of the Lake Albert Nyanza. 'For his own part, Sir Francis held that this rise and fall were mainly caused by the rapid growth of the tropical water-plants. During the dry season this vegetation increased enormously, and at the first rains large masses of aquatic growth were loosened by the rising of the waters. These masses, in the form of floating islands, passed downwards on the bosom of the flowing waters, and, on reaching a wide and shallow part of the river, gradually collected until they formed a dam of sufficient density to obstruct the progress of the river, and the water thus arrested found a temporary lodgment in the lake of Albert Nyanza, causing it to overflow its normal boundaries. At length the vegetable dam could no longer withstand the weight and pressure of the water bearing upon it. A portion gave way, a channel was opened, and the river, hurrying on to the sea, overflowed the banks of the Lower Nile, and drained the lake to a lower level. The fact was that the Albert Nyanza was nothing more than a huge backwater of the Upper Nile.'

It is right in connection with this subject to record the opinion lately expressed by Sir Samuel Baker, as to the possible cause of a protracted famine in Egypt. In the year 1888, great alarm was created by the low state of the Nile, and, in a letter to the *Times*, the distinguished traveller above named expressed himself thus on 'the necessity of keeping a firm hold upon the basin of the Nile, as an enemy in possession of the Blue Nile and the Atbara river could, by throwing a dam across the empty bed during the dry season, effectually deflect the stream when risen by the Abyssinian rains, and thus prevent the necessary flow towards Egypt.

'This might be effected in the Atbara river with the greatest ease, as the bed is perfectly dry during four or five months of the year, and all the necessary material is furnished for the dam by the fringe of forest upon the banks.

'Huge sacks made from the fibrous bark of the mimosa are manufactured in large quantities by the nomadic Arabs for the transport of gum-arabic; these are exactly suited as sand-bags for the formation of a dam, while the dôm palms and mimosas are present for piles and fascines. I have seen a spot, about 230 miles from the mouth of the Atbara, where the river might be deflected without difficulty, and be forced to an eastern course toward the Red Sea.

'This would be an engineering work well within the native capability. The Atbara, flowing east, would never reach the Red Sea, but it would inundate a vast area of desert lands, and render them fruitful, through a deposit of mud which now passes down to Lower Egypt. The Atbara river is the stream that has actually formed the Delta by the rich deposit of soil brought down from the fertile plains on the borders of Abyssinia. Without the Atbara river, Egypt would obtain only a scant supply of water, and would be certainly deprived of the fertiliz-ing element of the annual inundation.

'I have always believed, since I carefully examined

the river system of the Nile tributaries, that the seven years of famine in Lower Egypt during the time of Joseph were occasioned by a stoppage of the Atbara river; also of the Rahat and Dinder affluents of the Blue Nile.

'The Ethiopians were continually at war with the Egyptians, and they possessed the control of the Nile, by damming and deflecting the waters of those affluents. I do not presume to say that this was known to Joseph, who accordingly made the necessary arrangements for a great storage of provisions; but I can positively state that the plan is feasible, and that should any European be in command at the rebellious centre of the Soudan, his first strategical operation would be to deprive Egypt of the water that is necessary for her existence, and by the same means extend the fertile area of the rebel tribes.'

How far there may be truth in Sir Samuel Baker's conjecture as to this great famine I cannot presume to judge, but it seems evident that the distractions in Upper Egypt would be likely to throw much greater power into the hands of the rival potentates in Cush; and the study which I have devoted to the great Karnak list of tributary places and provinces in the south, of the date of Thothmes III., shows that in the victorious times which succeeded the expulsion of the Hyksôs, the Soudan, and Abyssinia, and Somâli land were the objects of great military attention on the part of the Pharaohs. But we must remember that other countries shared the drought.

CHAPTER VII.

JACOB AND HIS SONS.

WHEN the famine was so sore in the land of Canaan it was natural that Jacob should send his sons down into Egypt to buy corn. Many facile but superficial objections have been urged in detail against the likelihood of the narrative. Some of them have been so well anticipated by Dr. Thomson that I must quote a little by way of example[1] : 'When the crops of this country fail through drought or other causes, [he is speaking of South Palestine] the people still go down to Egypt to buy corn, as they did in the time of the patriarchs. It has also frequently occurred to me, when passing a large company of donkeys on their way to buy food, that we are not to suppose that only the eleven donkeys on which the brethren of Joseph rode composed the whole caravan. One man often leads or drives half a dozen ; and besides, I apprehend that Jacob's sons had many servants with them. Eleven sacks of grain, such as donkeys would carry, would not sustain a household like his for a week.

[1] *The Land and the Book*, p. 595.

It is no objection to this supposition that these servants
are not mentioned. There was no occasion to allude to
them, and such a reference would have disturbed the
perfect *unity* and touching simplicity of that most
beautiful narrative; and it is in accordance with the
general practice of Moses, in sketching the lives of the
patriarchs, not to confuse the story by introducing non-
historic characters. Thus, had it not been for the
capture of Lot by Chedorlaomer, we should not have
known that Abraham had three hundred and eighteen
full-grown men in his household; and so, also, had it not
been necessary for Jacob to send company after company
to guide his large presents to meet Esau, we might have
been left to suppose that he and his sons alone conducted
his flocks in his flight from Mesopotamia. But it is
certain that he had a large retinue of servants; and so,
doubtless, each of his sons had servants, and it is in-
credible that they should have gone down to Egypt
without them. On the contrary, there is every reason to
believe that there was a large caravan. The fact, also,
that the sons themselves took part in the work, and that
each had his sack under him, is in exact correspondence
with the customs of tent-dwelling shepherds at this day.
The highest sheikhs dress and fare precisely as their
followers do, and bear their full share in the operations of
the company, whatever they may be.'

We must always remember that the corn was carried
in quite a different thing (Heb. *k'li*, Gen. xlii. 25) from
that (*saq*) *sack* which contained the 'provender,' and in
which each man's money, and the silver cup, were secretly
put. The latter receptacle is also called by a third name,
viz. *amtakhath* (Gen. xlii. 27, 28, &c.), a word never

again occurring in Scripture. Yet learned professors put into the hands of young people such objections as the following : ' The whole world suffers from the famine, and is obliged to go to Egypt for corn. This is necessarily involved in the story, for why else should Jacob's sons have chosen Egypt for their second as well as their first purchase of corn? Is such a state of things credible in real life? Again, Jacob sends ten of his sons, each with his own ass, to buy corn. One cannot help asking why he did not send one son at the head of a caravan? What little provision was laid in in this way, however, cannot have gone far towards supporting the whole family, especially if, as we are told, part of it had to be used as fodder for the beasts by the way. And yet the story tells us distinctly that each of Jacob's sons took his own sack with him upon his own ass ; else, how could it be said that the cup was hidden and afterwards found in Benjamin's special sack?' And so on in the same vein.

Joseph accuses his brethren of coming as spies. Now it is interesting to find similar suspicious words in the mouth of Sekenen-Râ when Apepi's ambassador comes to him with his train : ' Who sent thee here to this city of the south? How hast thou come to spy out?' (*Papyrus Sallier*, I., so Brugsch translates). And the feeling of suspicion is expressed naturally enough. ' By the life of the Pharaoh,' was a well-known Egyptian oath. It is curious that *ankh* means 'to swear,' 'oath,' as well as ' life.' The accused takes an oath 'by the king's life ' not to speak falsely. A man swears 'by the name of the Pharaoh.' A workman in a necropolis had sworn by the name of the Pharaoh, and was reported by an officer to the prefect of the town. It was beyond the com-

petence of the subordinate, he said, to punish the workman for this offence. It would seem that great lords
might swear by the Pharaoh without rebuke :

> 'That in the captain's but a choleric word
> Which in the soldier is flat blasphemy.'

Certainly solemn and judicial use of oaths was com-
mended, but perjury and careless or wanton swearing
were prohibited, and included among sins in the 'Ritual'
of the Egyptians.

The employment of an interpreter at court was not
only natural and necessary, but we find it expressly
brought before us in Egyptian scenes ; as, for instance, in
that of the thirty-seven Asiatic foreigners introduced to
the Egyptian governor, to which we have before referred.
Here we see the interpreter, 'Khiti the scribe.' It is very
curious to find in the highly-important cuneiform tablets
lately discovered at Tel-al-Amarna, north of Thebes, and
dated between the time of Joseph and the Exodus, that
an interpreter is sent from Mesopotamia into Egypt, and
called *Targumanu*, a *dragoman*.

There is a small detail in the narrative of the intercourse between Joseph and his brethren which is at first
sight almost amusing. Joseph inquires : ' Is your father
well, the old man of whom ye spake ? Is he yet alive ? '
And they answered : ' Thy servant, our father, is in good
health ; he is yet alive.'

The inverted order, ' Is it peace to him ? Is he alive ? '
is very unusual ; but it seems also to be quite Egyptian.
Chabas gives us some most interesting extracts from
letters written in the time of Merenptah (probably the
time of Moses), by a lady in an Egyptian outpost in
Syria to friends at home in the Delta. In these familiar

communications the very phrase in question occurs more
than once. She writes : 'I am very well off; I am
alive;' and again, about a friend : 'His majesty's aide-
de-camp Setemua is in good plight ; he lives; don't
trouble yourself about him ; he is quartered with us at
Ta-makhirpé'—the garrison in question.

It is true that the Egyptians thought so much, and
with so little fear, of death and things beyond, that to
them the question, 'Is it peace to such an one?' might
not seem to render superfluous the further inquiry, 'Is he
alive?' Anyhow, this coincidence is to me very pleasing[1].

On the second journey of Joseph's brethren they took
with them, by their father's command, among their
presents, those very balms and aromatics which the
Midianite merchants were conveying into Egypt when
his brethren added Joseph to the merchandise of their
caravan. We have before explained what these spices
were.

The cup of Joseph's divination is worthy of note. The
Hebrew word נביע is used only in this passage, in
Exodus xxv, xxxvii, of the 'bowls,' (Revised Version,
'cups') of the golden candlestick ; and in Jeremiah
xxxv, of 'pots of wine' in the priests' chambers. I think
the word *kabu*, or *gabu*, in Egyptian 'blossom,' is equivalent to this. Compare ' *kabu* of wine[2].'

The beautifully-formed vessels of silver, as well as of
gold, brought as tribute by the Semitic Ruten folk
during the reigns of the XVIIIth Egyptian dynasty,
may well illustrate the probable character of Joseph's
cup of silver. In the museum of the Louvre, among the

---

[1] Chabas, *Mélanges*, 3ᵐᵉ série, t. ii. p. 152 ; also *Études, &c.*, p. 216.
[2] Pap. Harris, *Records of the Past*, vol. vi. p. 41.

very interesting relics of the great officer of Thothmes III., Tahutia, who figures in the marvellous adventure of the taking of Joppa[1], are two beautiful shallow cups, one of gold, the other of silver, like that of Joseph, of which 'the bottom is occupied by a flower with straight petals, around which swim five fishes in a sort of garland of lotus-blossoms[2].'

'As to the fact of divining by cups in Ancient Egypt there can be no doubt. It is mentioned by Iamblichus in his book on Egyptian mysteries (p. iii, sect. 14); and that the superstition descended to comparatively modern times appears from a circumstance mentioned in Norden's Travels (published in 1756). When he and his party were at Derri, on the confines between Egypt and Nubia, and in circumstances of great danger, they sent a threatening message to a malicious and powerful Arab. He replied, " I know what sort of people you are. *I have consulted my cup*, and have found by it that you are the people of whom one of our prophets has said, that Franks should come in disguise, and spy out the land; that they would afterwards bring a great number of their countrymen, conquer the land, and exterminate all," &c.[3]'

Vessels of silver are of very rare occurrence in Egypt, but it was a metal exceedingly valued and used by the Hittites.

The various turns and subtleties of this unequalled narrative have been carefully followed out and explained

---

[1] Maspero, *Comment Thoutii prit la ville de Joppé.*

[2] Pierret, *Salle Historique, &c.* p. 87. Ebers mentions the golden and silver diadem of an Antef of the XIth dynasty in the Museum at Leyden, and remarks that silver was more costly than gold in Ancient Egypt (*Aegypten und die Bücher Mose's*, p. 272).

[3] See Fairbairn's *Imperial Bible-Dictionary* (1886), v. art. ' Divination.'

by commentators. The mature experience of human nature which Joseph had gained enabled him like a sagacious physician to turn to good and kind account his special knowledge of the 'constitutions,' temperaments, and characters of his different brethren, and to lead them by singular expedients to ripen the good and cast off the evil qualities that marked them [1].

The way in which the nobler part of Judah's character was brought into growth and strength is a very fine part of the family story. Doubtless, too, the cruel and wrathful Simeon had time for reflection and self-discipline in the prison. And all the pitiful love of the elder

---

[1] In the Hulsean Lectures of the Rev. C. Benson on *Scripture Difficulties* (1822) are some excellent remarks on Joseph's conduct to his brethren. On the words ' he spake roughly,' &c., he comments thus : ' His last interview with them was at the pit ; his last request to them for his life : and it had failed. Reuben's prayers, and not his own, had saved him alive. . . . He must have been either more or less than a man, then, had he not retained the remains of a just and indignant remembrance of what he had experienced at their hands ' (p. 364). The author points out his ' desire to ascertain the present situation of his father and his family, especially of Benjamin, . . . who, as well as himself, was subject to their hatred.'

' The charge of being "spies" overthrew their caution. Joseph was informed of two most interesting facts,—his father was alive, and Benjamin. Yet there was ambiguity ; and Joseph was not satisfied, remembering their falsehood, especially with regard to Benjamin,—why had he not come? So to bring Benjamin, if alive, he took Simeon. On Benjamin alone his mind is fixed, he omits his father, we suppose he may scarcely have believed his father was alive,—they had only said "their youngest brother was that day with their father "—but where? In Canaan, or in the grave? When Simeon was taken, they said one to another, " We are verily guilty," &c.— the first words of sorrow for him ! The beginning of their penitence was the beginning of his tenderness, and he wept. Now he determined to *give* them the corn.'

I have given a sketch of part of the lecturer's interesting exposition, as a specimen of his treatment of the history. The student will do well to refer to the book and pursue the inquiry under such guidance.

brethren was drawn out towards Benjamin, while their jealousies and evil surmisings died away. So also the venerable patriarch, himself so refined in the furnace of trial, was gradually brought into due honour and authority in the course of all these elaborate vicissitudes, which the good providence of God and the persistent sagacity of Joseph were working out from stage to stage of this marvellous course of human training.

It is not my purpose to add one more exposition to those already available for instruction in these weighty matters, but rather to direct attention to the less frequented subjects in which we may learn from ancient sources, lately brought to light, both to understand and rightly to estimate these sacred records of 'the Scriptures of truth.'

We must now say something of the concentration of power in the hands of the Pharaoh which was brought about by Joseph; and here we cannot do better than translate from the very valuable work of M. l'Abbé Vigouroux [1]: 'What we know of property at a later period confirms the narrative of Genesis. The soil of Egypt, according to Diodorus Siculus, was divided in three parts, the first belonging to the priests, the second to the king, the third to the soldiers. The exemption of taxation in favour of the priests is mentioned in Genesis. There is no question of the soldiers, but their privilege may have been introduced later.' 'Herodotus tells us that they had the right to hold twelve *arurae* of land exempt from imposts, doubtless in lieu of pay. The mass of the population could not then become possessed of landed property.' 'In the sculptures,' says Wilkinson,

---

[1] *La Bible et les Découvertes Modernes*, 4me ed., p. 190 *et seqq.*

'we never see any except the kings, the priests, and the soldiers, as landowners.'

'Egyptology confirms indirectly the fact of the transference of property in the soil of Egypt to the Pharaohs, although we know not by whom it was made. It establishes, in fact, that under the ancient and the middle empire there existed a sort of feudal system, much like ours of the Middle Ages, often turbulent, and on many occasions little disposed to recognize the authority of the Pharaoh. The nomes were hereditary principalities committed to the hands of some great families, and allowed to pass from one to another by marriage or inheritance, on condition that the new possessor should obtain confirmation of his acquisition from the reigning sovereign [1].' 'Under the new empire after the Hyksôs, we no more meet any trace of this feudal organization. Joseph must have given it the last blow, by transferring to the king the property of all the country, the priestly domains alone excepted. Râmeses III., in the great Harris Papyrus, gives himself out as proprietor of the soil of Egypt.'

With regard to the organization and endowment of the military body by Râmeses II., M. Eugène Revillout has pointed out that the testimony of Diodorus is confirmed in an interesting manner by the celebrated poem of Pentaour on the great exploit of the Pharaoh at Kadesh on the Orontes, in the passage where Râmeses reproaches his soldiers for cowardice, and recounts the benefits that he had conferred upon their order [2].

[1] Ledrain, *Un Grand Seigneur Féodal, &c., Contemporain,* 1ʳᵉ Avril 1876.
[2] *Revue Egyptologique,* 1884, p. 101.

The Abbé Vigouroux has correctly observed, 'that the sacred writer does not say that the Pharaoh had the real and absolute property in the lands of the Egyptians; he leaves them to their old proprietors, exacting only that they should pay as a tax to him the fifth part of the income. This measure then amounts simply to the raising of a tribute.'

It is well worth while to study the details given by this learned writer on the subject of land tenure from Michaud ; and the vindication of the conduct of Joseph by the celebrated German scholar Ewald.

CHAPTER VIII.

JACOB'S MIGRATION.

I QUITE agree with what M. Naville has observed in a valuable article in the *Revue Chrétienne* for 1880[1]; 'Throughout the whole episode of the life of Joseph an attentive perusal of the Biblical narrative reveals a sort of separation between the king and his subjects, between the race of the conquerors, favourable to the foreign emigrants, and the home-born population. This separation was not, however, complete; we do not forget that the last Hyksôs kings had complied almost completely with the customs of Egypt, always preserving their own national god.'

These remarks apply very well to the details of those delightful scenes in which domestic and familiar life is so woven into the rich tapestry of courtly and royal pomp and circumstance, in the bringing of the patriarch Jacob, and his reception, and afterwards of his splendid obsequies.

In the Book of Genesis (xlvi. 28, 29) we are told that

[1] *Les Israélites en Egypte.*

Jacob 'sent Judah before him unto Joseph, to show the way before him unto Goshen; and they came into the land of Goshen. And Joseph made ready his chariot, and went up to meet Israel his father, to Goshen; and he presented himself unto him, and fell on his neck, and wept on his neck a good while.'

Those who have seen the admirable terra-cotta reliefs of Tinworth can never read this story without remembering those life-like groups in which he has revived, with such high genius, the scene of this great historic meeting.

The Septuagint version, written in Egypt, tells us that Judah went to meet Joseph at Hēroōnpolis, in the land of Ramesses, and that Joseph met Israel, his father, there. The Coptic version gives the name of the place as Pithom; and it turns out that all are right, for at Pi-tum M. Naville found Roman inscriptions bearing the name ERO, ERO CASTRA, the (Roman) camp Ero, and HPOϒ in Greek. The Greek HPOϒ well represents the Egyptian *Aru*, plural of *Ar*, 'magazine' or 'storehouse;' and this, as M. Naville believes, is the true derivation of the name, confirmed by the use of the word in inscriptions on the spot [1].

Now it is in this direction that a very ancient road across the desert from the south of Palestine leads, by which the patriarchs probably entered Palestine from Hebron and Beer-sheba. This was the belief of the late accomplished and experienced traveller, the Rev. F. W. Holland, who discovered this ancient way, which leads into Ismaïlieh from the East. Colonel Sir C. W. Wilson, R.E., has given a map of this route, with notes, in the

---

[1] *The Store-city of Pithom*, p. 6.

Palestine Exploration Fund's *Quarterly Statement* for 1884.

The advice which Joseph gave to his brethren, on which he and they acted so successfully, agrees very well with the conditions of the times of the Hyksôs, for it is clear that the shepherds were no abomination to the Pharaoh, although the Egyptians held them so. The 'best of the land' which was assigned to them in Goshen must have meant the best for herdsmen; and they were promoted to the office of stewards of the cattle of the Pharaoh in that part of the country which would bring them least in contact with the native Egyptians. Those who wish to study the interesting questions respecting the land of Goshen will turn to Dr. Ebers' elaborate work, *Durch Gosen zum Sinai*, 2nd ed., 1881, and the geographical matter given by Dr. Dümichen[1], and will find the information well digested by the Abbé Vigouroux. But M. Naville has carefully examined the data in the light of his own explorations in his memoir on *Saft el-Henneh and the Land of Goshen*, published by Trübner in 1887 for the Committee of the Egypt Exploration Fund. It has been a favourite and plausible notion that the name of Goshen was preserved, and the site of its capital indicated, by the Fakûs of these days, the Phacusa of Ptolemy, the first syllable being the Egyptian article Pa. But M. Naville has given his reasons for concluding that the village of Saft el-Henneh is the ancient capital of Goshen, Pa-Sopt, named after the tutelary god of the Nome of Arabia, of which this place was the sacred capital.

---

[1] *Geschichte des Altens Aegyptens*, in Oncken's series.

The village stands on the site of a large ancient city, once occupied by the Romans, and enclosed by massive walls of crude brick. There is still a great market held on the mound on Wednesdays [1]. M. Naville has closely studied the matter, and considers that the Goshen of the time of Joseph may be roughly reckoned as having its northern boundary from about the present railway junction of Zagazig, very near the ancient Bubastis (Pi-beseth of Scripture), nearly to Tel-el-Kebir, and that it extended southwards somewhat farther than Belbeis. He considers the expression 'land of Rameses' as covering a larger extent than Goshen. It included the city of Heroöpolis, discovered by M. Naville at Tel-el-Mas-khûta, where the station is, on the railway to Ismaïlia, which the French engineers called Ramses, following the mistaken identification with that store-city, whereas it was really Pithom.

'The traveller who leaves the station of Zagazig and journeys towards Tel-el-Kebir crosses, in all its width, what was the old land of Goshen. This part of the country is still particularly fruitful; it abounds in fine villages, the sheikhs, and even the common inhabitants, of which are generally very well off [2].'

In the old Pharaonic times the territory of the town of

---

[1] Saft is regarded by M. Naville as the true site of Phacusa, Pa-kes, as the place is twice called in the inscription on a shrine erected there by Necta-nebo II. (Nekhtnebef), and discovered by M. Naville, who is inclined to think that this is also the store-city Rameses, built by the enthralled Israelites for their great oppressor. It appears that Brugsch has given his adherence to the same identification at the Congress of Orientalists at Stockholm (*Academy*, 1889, p. 190).

Mr. Flinders Petrie, on geographical grounds, agrees in assigning the position of the Phacusa of Ptolemy to Saft el-Henneh (*Naukratis*, p. 91).

[2] Naville, *Theological Monthly*, 1889, p. 149.

Bubastis was called *sekhet nuter*, 'the divine meadow,'
and personified in the temple of Edfou under the figure
of a woman with an inscription which reads: 'The
meadow of the East, very beautiful, which bears the
flowers of the meadow *sekhet nuter* [1].'

Among the scraps of correspondence contained in the
celebrated Anastasi papyri, is one in which an officer
announces to Mineptah (or Merenptah), the probable
Pharaoh of Exodus, that 'we have let the tribes of the
Shasu (nomad Asiatics) of the country of Aduma,
pass the fortress Khetam of the King Mineptah-Hotep-
himât . . . which is in the country of Thuku, beside the
meres of the town Patum of the King Mineptah-Hotep-
himât, which is in the country of Thuku, to feed them
and to feed their cattle in the domain of the Pharaoh,
who is the good sun of all the world.' This refers to
an exactly similar admission of Eastern foreigners into
the land of Goshen through the route of Pithom in
the much later days when the children of Jacob in
their sore bondage had built the store-cities for the commissariat supplies of the Egyptian armies on their departure for Syria. But M. Naville brings down his notices
to the Middle Ages to establish the identity of the land
of Goshen.

Besides the Egyptian authorities, he gives information
derived from Arabic authors of note, and an extract from
the very curious narrative of a lady's pilgrimage in the
fourth century, lately found at Arezzo by Signor Gamur-
rini.

It is very clear that, whatever may have been the exact

---

[1] Brugsch, *Dict. Géog.* p. 13.

extent of the 'land of Goshen' at various times, we know what was the region occupied by the brethren of Joseph. And it is the more interesting to inquire into the antiquities of this district since M. Naville's last researches at Bubastis (Tel Basta) have for the first time revealed the fact that this was a chief residence of the later Hyksôs kings, at any rate, and, as it appears, we have now in the British Museum the fine sculpture-portrait of an Apepi, who, in the opinion of the learned Egyptologist, is none other than the Pharaoh of Joseph. At all events, the adjoining portal-jambs bear the inscription of that latter Apepi.

We may now think it likely that Joseph's chariot passed from Bubastis right through the land of Goshen to meet his father at the eastern post of that great highway to the desert and the land of Canaan, which has seen the march of so many armies since the time of the great Pharaohs of the XIIth dynasty down to the entrance of our own forces, guided by the stars to Tel-el-Kebir.

After meeting his father, Joseph proceeds to the court, to announce in person to the Pharaoh the arrival of his family and their retinue and possessions out of the land of Canaan: 'And, behold, they are in the land of Goshen,' he said; and he presented five of his brethren to the Pharaoh: 'And Pharaoh said unto his brethren, What is your occupation? And they said unto Pharaoh, Thy servants are shepherds, both we and our fathers. And they said unto Pharaoh, To sojourn in the land are we come; for there is no pasture for thy servants' flocks; for the famine is sore in the land of Canaan; now, therefore, we pray thee, let thy servants dwell in the land of

Goshen.' And Pharaoh spake unto Joseph, saying:
'Thy father and thy brethren are come unto thee; the
land of Egypt is before thee ; in the best of the land make
thy father and thy brethren to dwell ; in the land of
Goshen let them dwell ; and if thou knowest any men of
activity among them, then make them rulers over my
cattle.'

That to the *Egyptians* every shepherd was an abomination was a consideration that would lead to the family of
Joseph remaining where they already were, in Goshen,
'the best of the land.' If by 'Egyptians' are meant the
native race of Mizraïm, as distinct from the Hyksôs
and mixed people of the Delta (as Potiphar was noted
'an Egyptian'), then the reasoning is plain, and would
prevent Joseph's kinsfolk from being sent up the country.
Thus also the way of retreat to their own land would
be open to them in case of need ; and they would be
best able to gain intelligence from those parts, and, of
course, to maintain constant intercourse with Joseph
himself.

The Pharaoh kindly enters into the plan. They were
no abomination to him, as his whole demeanour towards
them plainly testified ; and this helps to show that he
was of Asiatic race.

Now the care of the royal cattle of Egypt was no slight
matter, for we know from the monuments that even in
the far earlier times when the Pyramids were built, the
possessions of high nobles included herds and flocks of great
number and beauty. They were most carefully treated,
fed and housed, nursed and doctored, and everything
relating to them was methodically taken down in writing
and duly reported. The royal herds at the time of Joseph

too were largely increased, as the Scripture narrative tells us, by the acquisition of the cattle which were brought in exchange for grain ; therefore a great and goodly prospect of business and responsibility lay open before the most capable of Joseph's brethren. After this prosperous commencement, Joseph next presents his aged father himself. 'And Joseph brought in Jacob, his father, and set him before Pharaoh, and Jacob blessed Pharaoh. And Pharaoh said unto Jacob : How many are the days of the years of thy life ? And Jacob said unto Pharaoh : The days of the years of my sojournings are a hundred and thirty years ; few and evil have been the days of the years of my life, and they have not attained unto the days of the years of the life of my fathers, in the days of their sojournings. And Jacob blessed Pharaoh, and went out from the presence of Pharaoh.' It is worth while to give, in view of the age of Jacob, some veritable instances of extreme longevity, both ancient and modern.

In July, 1882, Lord Talbot de Malahide read a paper on the longevity of the Romans in North Africa, in which he 'gave several instances of epitaphs and inscriptions on tombs of persons whose age had exceeded a hundred years, in some cases an age of 120, 130, and even 140 years had been attained.'

In the *Lancet* of September, 1883, is a circumstantial account of an old woman in a village called Auberives-en-Royans, between Valence and Grenoble, who had reached the age of 123 years, 'with no infirmity except slight deafness, being in full possession of her mental faculties.' This is confirmed in the *Morning Post* of October 6, 1883, by a letter from the *maire* of the place, who says: 'It is quite true our centenarian is 123 years of age, and the hundredth anniversary of her marriage was the 13th of last January. She still remembers starting with her husband for the war under the first empire. She possesses the use of all her faculties except hearing, and is even able to do the little cooking she requires, and to keep her little room very clean.'

Another instance of extreme age is given in the *Morning Post* of February 4, 1888, in a Reuter's telegram dated February 3: 'The Pope to-day received the Scholars and Professors of the College of the Propaganda. Monseigneur Adaux, from California, presented to his holiness a photograph of Gabriel, the Indian Catholic, who is now aged 140 years, and requested a special benediction for him.'

It is a curious thing that Berosus, the Chaldæan historian, gives 116 years as the ideal length of life. We shall see hereafter that the Egyptians traditionally held a shorter age as their desired lifetime.

What would we give for a faithful portraiture of Abraham, Jacob, or Joseph? The general type of their features we may indeed fairly project before our imagination, by the help of those most interesting mural paintings in Egyptian tombs, which our artists have given to us in the great works of Champollion, Rosellini, and Lepsius.

It is indeed a wonderful thing that the aspect of the great oppressor at whose court Moses was brought up is perfectly familiar to us in its growth from boyhood to maturity through innumerable statues and portraits; and lastly, the very 'statue of flesh,' his own embalmed body, has been brought from the darkness of the tomb, to show us the actual face on which the great Hebrew so often gazed.

We have not, indeed, the same opportunity of verifying the counterfeit presentments of Merenptah, but we have most artistic likenesses of that monarch.

And if M. Naville is right, the most interesting, and perhaps the most beautifully executed Egyptian royal head in the British Museum, gives us the authentic features of Joseph's Pharaoh.

It wears the familiar folded head-dress of the Egyptian monarchs, and the royal basilisk on the forehead. The face is most interesting, for it is a refined and dignified version of the type presented by the sphinxes of Sân.

The countenance is of squarish frame, with high cheek-bones, the cheeks themselves rather sunk, the mouth and lower jaw prominent, but well-formed, and the chin finely rounded up to the slightly projecting lower lip, with a very firm, but not surly, look. The nose, rather injured, is well-proportioned and handsomely formed; the eyes, well apart, are denoted by cavities intended for the wonderful work in some different material which only Egyptian artists would employ; but in the absence of their orbits there is a proud and calm expression of intellect.

We see in this fine face something of Egyptian serenity, but without the attractive cheer of that well-favoured nation.

The twin statues unearthed by M. Naville at Bubastis may have stood in the temple at the time of which we are speaking, and it does not seem unlikely that the introduction of Jacob and his sons to the Pharaoh may have taken place in that important city, whose ruins are only second in dignity to those of Zoan.

We have already spoken of the administration of public affairs by Joseph. It is evident that his purpose was the centralisation of power; and we must remember that, far from being the rigid and unchanging system which is popularly supposed, the government of Egypt had passed through many violent changes, dislocations, and vicissitudes, some of which are known to us, and many more may be inferred as probable. At the time there were impending civil wars, which eventually issued in the total overthrow of the foreign domination. There were also strong hereditary princes to be kept under discipline and in unity, and when the mass of the people became lieges of the Pharaoh, they were simply doing homage to him as their lord, and gaining the same sort of advantages that our forefathers obtained by the wise concentration of power under King Alfred, and our fellow-subjects in India now enjoy by the overthrow of the sanguinary despots of different and rival races, whose exactions and tyrannies hindered all true developments or progress.

How great and surprising was the expansion of Egyptian power under the vigorous native Pharaohs of the great XVIIIth dynasty we are only now learning from the cuneiform records of Tel-el-Amarna.

The Israelites took good root in Goshen, 'and they gat them possessions therein, and were fruitful, and multiplied exceedingly.' And evidently the stronger did they grow, so much the stronger grew the Pharaoh

in devoted lieges, 'men of activity,' and fit in every way
for his service [1].

[1] In the *Zeitschrift für Aeg. Spr.* 1889, p. 125, Dr. E. von Bergmann
describes an injured block of relief-sculpture in the Imperial Museum at
Berlin, of the time of Har-em-heb, the last king of the great XVIIIth
dynasty. The tableau represents a company of Egyptians bending forward
submissively with hands on knees. A single man follows them in the same
attitude. Similar groups occur at Tel-el-Amarna. The inscription, of
which the beginning is much marred, seems to relate to a troop of Semitic
immigrants who are come to honour 'the good god, the great and mighty,
Har-em-heb.' They are called *Menti-u* (the name applied to nomads, and
to the Hyksôs), and it appears that their enemies had destroyed and wasted
their town by fire; 'their lands hunger; they live as the wild beasts of the
deserts.' Some of the barbarians who knew not how to live were come (it
apparently says) to the Pharaoh, 'as was the usage of the father of their
fathers from the beginning;' and they are received and committed to the
care of officers, that they may keep within the boundaries assigned to them
(cf. *Pr. S. B. Arch.* 1889, p. 425). This very interesting record seems very
similar to the much later narrative of the admission of the Shasu in the time
of Mer-en-ptah to pasture their herds within the defensive eastern frontier of
the Delta, and both remarkably illustrate the Scripture narrative.

CHAPTER IX.

THE DYING ISRAEL.

IT was seventeen years after the entrance of Joseph's family into Egypt that 'the time drew near that Israel must die:' and he called his son Joseph, and exacted from him an oath, after the manner of his people, not to bury him in Egypt, but, when he should sleep with his fathers, to carry him out of Egypt and bury him in their burying-place. 'And he [Joseph] said, I will do as thou hast said. And he said, Swear unto me: and he sware unto him.'

Then we come to a highly interesting and significant point in the narrative. For we are told that when Joseph sware, Israel bowed himself על־ראש המטה. Now, if we take the Epistle to the Hebrews for our guide, we must render these words ἐπὶ τὸ ἄκρον τῆς ῥάβδου αὐτοῦ, upon (or towards) the top of his staff. But our Authorised Version and Revised Version render, 'upon the bed's head.' The Epistle to the Hebrews follows the Septuagint. The variation arises from the fact that the same word in Hebrew means either bed or staff,

according to the vowel sounds with which it is pronounced. As we have the passage written and printed
now, it stands הַמִּטָּה, the bed ; not הַמַּטֶּה staff.

It will be observed that we are not informed whose
staff is in question. It has often been referred to
Joseph's, and not to Jacob's own staff.

This explanation has been repudiated with good
reason, if it were supposed that the bowing down implied
a religious act of worship to the head of Joseph's staff.
Nevertheless, it is worth while to enquire whether there
was not a solemn interchange of mutual reverence.
The son Joseph obeys his father's behest by swearing
to fulfil his injunction and bury him in the sepulchre
of Abraham at Hebron. But in making that request
Jacob had observed a ceremonial reverence as towards
a lord; 'If now I have found grace in thy sight,'—
being evidently mindful of the high place of authority
held by Joseph, which, indeed, was ultimately manifested
by the royal pomp of the obsequies accorded to Jacob.

Whose then was the staff in question, to the head
of which Jacob bowed himself down ? If Joseph's, it
was the symbol of the high authority of the deputy
of the Pharaoh, the lord over all the land of Egypt,
at whose mouth every one should kiss, as we have before
explained : and Jacob might well remember his own
old incredulous question ;—' Should he indeed come to
bow down himself to Joseph ? '

It would be an act of homage rendered in express
fulfilment of the Divine prognostic given in the dream
of Joseph's boyhood.

This explanation receives a new and striking light
from the researches of the late eminent Egyptologist

Chabas [1]. He explains the use of the head of the staff in making oath by touching that part of the symbol of authority in the hand of the ruler, in token of homage. This is also the decided opinion of Mr. Reginald Stuart Poole [2].

The great French Orientalist, de Sacy, had explained the passage in Heb. xi. 21 in the same manner. In a note he writes: 'The sense is; that by this act of outward reverence which Jacob rendered to the staff of Joseph, he honoured his power and the dignity that he possessed in Egypt, and that he adored in the spirit of faith the power of the kingdom of Jesus Christ, of which the staff of Joseph was the figure.'

I believe Calvin inclined to the same opinion. We may notice as an illustration that Râmeses II. touches the outstretched sceptre of Amen-Râ in offering to a triad of Egyptian gods. It is the act of homage so familiar in the history of Esther, when the Persian king holds out the golden sceptre.

The patriarch had indeed blessed the Pharaoh who was worshipped by his own subjects as a veritable god—but here, where no profanation could be supposed, Jacob renders homage to the Pharaoh's vicegerent in the person of his own long-lost son.

The staff of office wielded by Egyptian potentates may be seen in the British Museum, made of ebony or other wood, and its head of ivory, carved as a papyrus flower or otherwise.

Dr. Ebers gives [3] a strange tradition of the Arabs with

[1] *Sur l'usage des bâtons de main* (Lyon, 1875, p. 10). *Mélanges égyptal*, série iii. tome 1, p. 80.

[2] *Contemporary Review*, 1879, p. 753.

[3] *Durch Gosen zum Sinai*, p. 579.

regard to the staff wielded by a succession of patriarchs from Adam to Moses, and a Rabbinical story of the same complexion about the wonderful staff inherited by Jacob from Adam, and given by him to Joseph.

It is an interesting thing that at Hebron, in the sepulchral chamber where it is said that Joseph was ultimately buried, a staff is hung up [1].

It does not seem that Jacob had been especially ill when he exacted that solemn promise from his son; but infirmity and blindness had warned him of his approaching departure. Next we find that one 'told Joseph, Behold, thy father is sick: and he took with him his two sons, Manasseh and Ephraim. And one told Jacob, and said, Behold, thy son Joseph cometh unto thee: and Israel strengthened himself, and sat upon the bed. And Jacob said unto Joseph, God Almighty (*El Shaddai*) appeared unto me at Luz in the land of Canaan, and blessed me, and said unto me, Behold, I will make thee fruitful, and multiply thee, and I will make of thee a company of peoples; and will give this land to thy seed after thee for an ever-lasting possession. And now thy two sons, which were born unto thee in the land of Egypt before I came unto thee into Egypt, are mine; Ephraim and Manasseh,

---

[1] Stanley, *History of the Jewish Church*, new ed. 1883, vol. i. p. 443.

Those who may wish to examine more minutely the matter of the Egyptian ceremonial of the staff will find details as follows: Birch, *Revue Archéologique*, 1ᵣᵉ série, tome xvi, 1859, p. 257; Maspero, *Une Enquête Judiciaire, &c.*, Paris, 1871; Devéria, *Le Pap. judiciaire de Turin, &c.*; Pierret, *Vocabulaire*, pp. 369, 405, 701; Erman, *Zeitschrift für Aegyptische Sprache*, 1879, p. 83. But I believe the result above indicated is not really affected, and I could give reasons for this conclusion, if this were the right place to do so.

even as Reuben and Simeon, shall be mine.' The two
sons of Joseph and Asenath, born before Jacob's arrival,
should rank as Jacob's own sons, equal to his eldest-born,
Reuben and Simeon; but any other children of Joseph
should reckon as belonging to them, not as forming
other tribes.

Ephraim and Manasseh are already mentioned by
Jacob in reverse order,—the younger first—thus showing
the deliberation of his purpose to prefer the younger.
Dr. Kalisch has treated this matter in a very interesting way [1].

'Joseph hastened to him from the royal residence,
stimulated partly by filial love, and partly by the desire
of conferring with him on a subject of the very highest
moment for the future of his house.

'He had married an *Egyptian* wife, and had by her
during his separation from his relatives, and in a foreign
land, become the father of his two first-born sons, therefore, not groundlessly apprehending that his children
might be excluded from the hopes and the promised
inheritance of the Hebrews, he brought Ephraim and
Manasseh, then about 20 years old (comp. xli. 50), before
Jacob, in order to obtain his pledge of their unqualified
admission as members of his family (xlviii. 1). But these
thoughts had occupied Jacob not less seriously than
Joseph. When he, therefore, was informed of his son's
visit, he was determined finally to arrange the matter
(ver. 2). In order to prove that he was invested with
the lawful authority for unrestricted decision, he mentioned the manifestation of God which . . . had

---

[1] *Commentary on the Old Testament*, English ed. 1858.

been granted to him at Bethel, in confirmation of a
Divine vision before accorded to him at the same place,
when on his flight from Canaan to Mesopotamia (xxxv.
11, 12 ; comp. xxviii., 13-15). In virtue of the blessings
which he then received, as the spiritual heir of Abraham
and Isaac, he was enabled to bestow blessings on his own
descendants ; and in virtue of the promise which was then
made to him regarding the possession of Canaan, he was
entitled to divide the land among his progeny, according
to his own option (xlviii. 3, 4). He, therefore, adopted the
two eldest sons of Joseph, securing to them in every
respect equal rights with his own sons, and appointing
them as the chiefs over their younger brothers (ver. 5, 6).
Thus Joseph obtained from his father even more than
he had intended to solicit.'

'*Mine*,' — so Ainsworth explains, — 'as my next
children, and not my child's children. So these two are
made heirs by adoption with Jacob's sons, and Joseph
hath a double portion, the first birthright being taken
from Reuben and given unto him (Gen. xlix. 3, 4 ; 1
Chron. v. 1, 2), and of Joseph are reckoned two tribes,
both in the Prophets and Evangelists ; (Num. i. 32, 34 ;
Rev. vii. 6, 8).'

Then the aged Jacob finds utterance for the great
sorrow of all his 'few and evil' days : 'And as for me,
when I came from Padan, Rachel died by me in the land
of Canaan in the way, when there was still some way
to come unto Ephrath : and I buried her there in the
way to Ephrath.' 'Rachel died by me,' or 'for me,'
for, as Lange says : '‎עלי would mean, literally, *for him* ;
she died for him, since, while living she shared with him,
and for him, the toils of his pilgrimage life, and through

this, perhaps, brought on her deadly travail.' That this was so seems very likely, as we have before shown.

'Then,' as Lange well says, 'the old dim-eyed patriarch interrupts himself. He now perceives for the first time that he is not alone with Joseph, and asks, "Who are these?" "And Joseph said unto his father: They are my sons, whom God hath given me here. And he said, Bring them, I pray thee, unto me, and I will bless them. Now the eyes of Israel were dim for age, so that he could not see, and he brought them near unto him; and he kissed them, and embraced them. And Israel said unto Joseph, I had not thought to see thy face; and, lo, God hath let me see thy seed also. And Joseph brought them out from between his knees, and he bowed himself with his face to the earth. And Joseph took them both, Ephraim in his right hand toward Israel's left hand, and Manasseh in his left hand toward Israel's right hand, and brought them near unto him. And Israel stretched out his right hand, and laid it upon Ephraim's head, who was the younger, and his left hand upon Manasseh's head, guiding his hands wittingly (or crossing his hands); for Manasseh was the firstborn." Let us remark that it next says: " And he blessed Joseph, and said, The God before whom my fathers Abraham and Isaac did walk, the God which hath fed me all my life long unto this day, the Angel which hath redeemed me from all evil, Bless the lads; and let my name be named on them, and the name of my fathers Abraham and Isaac; and let them grow into a multitude in the midst of the earth." Here we will note that the Hebrew rendered " before whom" reminds us of the name Penuel; that the word

"fed" imperfectly denotes the ruling, guiding, and protect-
ing work of the shepherd, which is intended, as in
Psalm xxiii. And that the last and the first clause of
this sublime and beautiful invocation are shown in connexion in "the Angel of His presence" (מלאך פניו) of
Isaiah lxiii. 9.'

'It is worthy of notice,' says Lange, 'that, along
with this threefold meaning of God (which would seem
to sound like an anticipation of the Trinity [1], there
is, at the same time, clearly presented the conception
of God's presence, of His care as a Shepherd, and of
His faithfulness as Redeemer, — all too in connexion
with the laying on of hands.'

We have, therefore, in this passage a point in which
the revelation makes a significant advance : ' And when
Joseph saw that his father laid his right hand upon the
head of Ephraim, it displeased him : and he held up his
father's hand, to remove it from Ephraim's head on
to Manasseh's head. And Joseph said unto his father,
Not so, my father, for this is the firstborn ; put thy
right hand upon his head. And his father refused, and
said, I know it, my son, I know it : he also shall become
a people, and he also shall be great : howbeit his
younger brother shall be greater than he, and his seed
shall become a multitude of nations. And he blessed
them that day, saying, In thee shall Israel bless, saying,
God make thee as Ephraim and Manasseh : and he
set Ephraim before Manasseh.'

'This blessing,' as Keil observes, 'begins to fulfil
itself from the days of the Judges onwards ; as the
tribe of Ephraim in power and compass so increased

[1] See *Keil*, p. 281.

that it became the head of the northern ten tribes, and its name became of like significance with that of Israel; although in the time of Moses Manasseh still outnumbered Ephraim by 20,000' (Numb. xxvi. 34, 37).

'And Israel said unto Joseph, Behold, I die: but God shall be with you, and bring you again unto the land of your fathers. Moreover I have given to thee one portion above thy brethren, which I took out of the hand of the Amorite with my sword and with my bow.'

There is here a characteristic play upon the word rendered 'portion,' namely *shekem* ('shoulder,' or 'mountain-slope,' R.V. *marg.*), referring doubtless to the beautiful and fertile place where Jacob had purchased a possession, which he seems to have afterwards recovered from the Khivvites (Hivites of our version), who are here called by the great inclusive name Amorites.

The Septuagint version translates, 'I give thee Sikima' (Σίκιμα), the local name.

What was meant by Jacob in saying that he had taken this possession out of the hand of the Amorite with his sword and with his bow has been disputed. Some have thought he referred to the treacherous outrage of Simeon and Levi, which he so indignantly repudiates; some to an unmentioned forcible recovery of the land that he had purchased from Khamor.

But it is also viewed as a prophetic and future warrant for the possession of the district, as indeed came to pass. 'The perfect, לָקַחְתִּי, is used in a prophetic sense,' as Lange says; and Jacob views himself as the future people Israel.

It is well worth while, however, to read the argument of the late Bishop Wordsworth on the passage in Stephen's speech (Acts vii) relating to this matter. In verses 15, 16, it is said, 'So Jacob went down into Egypt, and died, he, and our fathers, and were carried over into Sychem, and laid in the sepulchre that Abraham bought for a sum of money of the sons of Emmor (the father) of Sychem.' Thus it is translated in the Authorized Version.

It is objected that Jacob was buried in the Makpelah at Hebron. The Greek reads, καὶ ἐτελεύτησεν αὐτὸς καὶ οἱ πατέρες ἡμῶν καὶ μετετέθησαν εἰς Συχέμ, καὶ ἐτέθησαν ἐν τῷ μνήματι ᾧ ὠνήσατο Ἀβραὰμ τιμῆς ἀργυρίου παρὰ τῶν υἱῶν Ἐμμὼρ τοῦ Συχέμ. Bishop Wordsworth replies that it is not said that Jacob was taken to Sychem, but that the fathers (heads of the tribes) were, and quotes two passages in which Jerome says that the fathers were buried there.

He also argues that, as Abraham built an altar there, he probably would have bought ground for that purpose, as Jacob afterwards did, and that it was this sacred possession that Jacob himself recovered by force from the Amorite and specially granted to Joseph. He urges moreover that Ἐμμὼρ τοῦ Συχέμ would properly mean (not the father, but) the son of Sychem, and that as there was a Khamor at Sychem five centuries later than Jacob's time (Judges ix. 28), the name was a hereditary title of the rulers of the place.

The Sinaitic Codex rids us of this subordinate question of τοῦ Συχέμ by reading Ἐμμωρ ἐν Συχεμ, which is followed by our Revised Version: 'Jacob went down into Egypt; and he died, himself, and our fathers; and they were

carried over unto Shechem, and laid in the tomb that
Abraham bought for a price in silver of the sons of
Hamor (Gr. Emmor) in Shechem.'

In the Book of Joshua (xxiv. 32) it is said that Joseph
was buried in Shekem, 'in the parcel of ground which
Jacob bought of the sons of Hamor, the father of Shechem,' &c.   It seems most probable that Khamor was a
hereditary title used by the Amorites.

The enigmatic expression of Jacob, 'one Shekem,'
may possibly, in connexion with Bishop Wordsworth's
remarks on Abraham's purchase and that of Jacob,
suggest that there were twin Shekems, which would
account for the plural form Σίκιμα in the Septuagint.

CHAPTER X.

'JACOB-EL AND JOSEPH-EL.'

WE have now to speak of a supposed trace of both Jacob and Joseph in an Egyptian record of the highest interest.

In the celebrated list of 119 names of places in Palestine tributary to Thothmes III., at Karnak, the 102nd name is 𓈖𓈖𓂝𓎡𓃀 𓃭𓇯 which in Hebrew letters would stand probably as יעקבאל (Jacob-el). It was de Rougé who first suggested the Hebrew transcription, and asked the question: 'Is it allowable to suppose that this name of locality preserves a memorial of one of the establishments of Jacob in Palestine?' Others have since treated this question, and especially, with remarkable ability, M. Groff[1]. The parallel name 𓈖𓈖𓈙𓃀𓇯, יספאל (Joseph-el), occurs as the 78th in the same list. We must now try to explain the inquiry, as it stands at present, as clearly as may be, and show its bearings on the life of Joseph. With regard to the last syllable in these two names, the hieroglyphic signs will very well represent the Hebrew אל, *el*, 'god.' This is borne out by other ex-

---

[1] *Revue Egyptologique*, 1885, pp. 95, &c., 146, &c., and 1886.

amples.   Then in the first name the transliteration יעקב,
Jacob, is exact, and Jacob-el would be the full form of
the name, similar to Isra-el and Ishma-el; and let us
take as an example of both forms יפתח (Jephthakh), both
a local name (Joshua xv. 43) and a well-known name of
a hero, and יפתח־אל (Jephthakh-el), a valley (Joshua xix.
14, 27), which is itself paralleled by the modern Arabic
local name of a ford, Makhâdet Fatah Allah.   'The
expression Fatah-Allah, or more commonly in vulgar
Arabic Yeftah-Allah, "may God open," is used when
looking forward to some piece of luck, as the first money
taken by a tradesman, &c.[1]'   The ford crosses the
Jordan about one-third of the way between the Sea of
Galilee and the Dead Sea[2].   We have exactly the same
form as Joseph-el in Joseph-Iah (Ezra viii. 10), יוספיה.

It may be objected that in the Egyptian hieroglyphs
we have the equivalent of שׁ, and in the name of Joseph
ס.   But this is probably only a dialectic variation, as in
the celebrated case of shibbôleth, which the Ephraimites
softened into ס, s ; as M. Groff has well observed.

The use of apocopated names is known in Egyptian
and Assyrian as well as in Hebrew.   Schrader gives, for
example, the name Isammi' as an abridged form of
Ishma-el[3].   I refer the student to a valuable article on
Egyptian proper names by M. Groff in the *Revue Egyptologique*, 1887, p. 86, &c.   I cannot agree with him,
however, in thinking that the Jacob-el and Joseph-el of
the Karnak List of Palestine are necessarily, or probably,
tribal names as distinguished from local names.   To
'call their lands after their own names' was such an

---

[1] *Pal. Survey, Name Lists*, p. 202.   [2] *Great Map*, sheet xii. Qm.
[3] *Eng. Tr.* vol. i. p. 135.

established and ancient custom, that there is no difficulty
in it. And in the case of the generality of these names
of the tribute-lists, it is hard to imagine any doubt of
their local character. This source of information has
not yet been taken into account by Biblical scholars in
any adequate way in its bearing on the narrative of the
Old Testament. Here we have 119 names, of which all
but a very few belong to Palestine, written by an
Egyptian scribe in hieroglyphic about the year 1600 B.C.,
something more than a century after the death of Jacob,
and almost in the noonday height of prosperity of the
great XVIIIth dynasty.

In a philological point of view, as the Vicomte Emma-
nuel de Rougé writes: 'This list of peoples conquered
by Thothmes III. in Syria presents an immense interest,
for it belongs to one of the questions which has been
most debated in Biblical studies, to wit, the origin of
the sacred language. What is it in fact but Hebrew?
If one believes the scholars of the last century, this will
be nothing else than the language of the race of Abraham; that, consequently, which the patriarch would
have brought with him. Critics bid us notice that Jacob,
on arriving, found all the names of towns and personages
written in the language called Hebrew, and that from
this fact we must conclude that this language was rather
that of Canaan. Just at first we cried out, and yet the
Bible itself contradicts the first theory, for when Jacob
raised the cairn of witness he gave it two names, the one
in Chaldee, the other in *Hebrew* [viz. 'Laban called it
Jegar-sahadutha: but Jacob called it Galeëd,' in Aramaic
and Hebrew equally meaning 'the heap of witness'].
The monument of the conquered peoples at Karnak

affords an important light on this debate. We are at
the moment when Jacob is in Palestine. It was, then,
at that time the true ancient name that is given on the
Egyptian monument ; now all the roots report themselves as Semitic, and the forms are Hebraic. So then,
at this epoch, the language of the country was that which
we have since called Hebrew, mingled naturally, according to the localities, with Aramaean or Arabic dialects[1].'

In fact, the transliteration into the Hebrew alphabet
gives us very generally the names as we have them in
the Old Testament ; and on the other hand the names
still current in the mouths of the inhabitants, as recorded
by the officers and scholars of the Palestine Survey,
equally bear out the trustworthiness and antiquity of the
Book of Joshua and other Biblical data of the early
times of Israel.

We cannot here, of course, enter on detailed inquiry
of this kind, but quite enough may be adduced to
illustrate what has been said[2].

But it is right to mention that I have added, I believe
with good reason, two groups of names to former identi-
fications, the one in the mountain-country of Ephraim,
the other surrounding the great sacred stronghold of
Hebron.

The name next preceding Joseph-el in the list is Har,
which I would identify with the celebrated upland dis-

---

[1] *Mélanges d'Archéologie Egyptienne et Assyrienne,* vol. ii. p. 99.

[2] The lists *in extenso,* which I have edited for the *Transactions of the Society
of Biblical Archaeology,* will be published in the next volume. They have
been treated with characteristic learning and ability by Professor Maspero
in the *Transactions of the Victoria Institute,* and previously by the lamented
Mariette, Major Conder, R.E., and others. They will appear, as edited by
me, in the new Series of *Records of the Past,* vol. v.

trict so well-known as Mount Ephraim, הר אפרים. 'An expression,' says Canon Tristram, 'which comprises all the hilly region from within a few miles north of Jerusalem at Bethel, as far as the plain of Esdraelon, including therefore the whole of the west allotment of Manasseh. Mount Ephraim was to the northern country what the hill country of Judah was to the southern—the backbone, centre, and strength of the nation.'

Rising on the east from the Jordan valley, this block of high land sinks down into the plain about Hadîthah, the Hadid of the Bible, חריד. The present name is in exact conformity with the hieroglyphic.

The place before this in the list is Naun, Nûn, a very interesting name, which still haunts the district north and south of Jebel et-Teyi, which I take as identical with the district of Taïa, immediately preceding it in the list. Within three or four miles are Jefa Nûn, Neby Nûn, a sacred place to the east of Yanûn, and, twelve miles further west, is the celebrated place where Nûn, the father of Joshua, is said to be buried near his illustrious son in the outskirts of Kefr Haris[1].

Jerome says that the holy lady Paula, who visited Timnath-serah, wondered that Joshua, who was the ruler of Israel, and the distributer of all the inheritances of the tribes, chose only a rough mountain tract of country for himself. But it may be that he chose the inheritance of his fathers, which bore the name of a great ancestor of his own. The family had, perhaps, possessions here, to which they returned with their great leader, a prince of Ephraim. At all events, the name Nûn was borne by a district in this region when Thothmes subjugated the

[1] *Pal. Survey, Mem.* vol. ii. p. 285.

country, some three centuries before ' they buried him in the border of his inheritance in Timnath-serah, which is in mount Ephraim, on the north side of the hill of Gaäsh.'

These places, occurring with Joseph-el in the tribute-list, I have included, in order to show that we are led to the mountains of Ephraim in seeking a local habitation for that interesting name. And if Har be indeed Har Ephraim, then our Joseph-el may linger in Yasûf, anciently called Yusepheh, and known as Yasûf in the Samaritan Book of Joshua [1].

Yasûf, with its wady, is not five miles east of Kefr Hâris and Neby Nûn. Yusephel may have been softened into Yusepheh, as Ekrebel (Judith vii. 18) into Akrabeh [2]; Irpeel into Râfat [3]; and Jabneel into Yebnah.

The description of Yâsûf in the *Memoirs* would suit a place of importance in early times. It is an 'ancient village in a valley, with a good spring in the village, and olives. A beautiful garden of pomegranates exists north of the spring. The water comes out of a cleft in a cliff, near which is an ancient well with steps. There is a sacred place, with a large oak (Sindian), and a ruined shrine, south-west of the village, near 'Ain er Raja. There are drafted stones in many houses, and remains of well-built enclosures now ruined. Many well-cut rock tombs are also found on either side.'

There is a Wady Yâsuf over the hill to the north. Now we turn to the name of Jacob-el, which occurs as

---

[1] *Palestine Survey*; sheet xiv. mp.; *Memoirs*, vol. ii. p. 287. *Name Lists*, p. 250. Neubauer, *Géog. du Talmud*, p. 90.

[2] *Handbook of the Bible*, p. 290.   [3] *Ibid*, Index, p. 415.

No. 102 of our list, and appears to belong to a region farther south.

At all events, it seems that we have the names of Jacob and of Joseph in Palestine at this early period; of Jacob somewhere in the southern region, and of Joseph in that very ' Mount Ephraim ' where his heirs strengthened their power on their return from captivity in Egypt.

The historical setting of these data has been thus given by M. Groff: 'We ask ourselves naturally how these data agree with history. The tradition places the descent of Israel into Egypt under one of the Shepherd-kings, which it names Aphobis. It is evidently one of the Apapis; it was probably under a king of the same name that the national war of independence broke out.

'Under Amosis the Shepherds were expelled and the XVIIIth dynasty was founded, of which the great Thothmes III. figures as the sixth king. Under his reign we see the coalition against him of Canaanite tribes, among whom we find the tribes of Jacob-el and Joseph-el. After the fall of the XVIIth dynasty was founded the XIXth, with Râmeses.

' It was probably under Râmeses II. that, according to the Biblical narrative, Moses was born, and under his son and successor Merenphtah that the Exodus took place. There we find the Hebrews divided into twelve tribes, of whom ten came directly from the patriarch Jacob, and the two others belonged to Joseph. Thus we see the perfect agreement of our hieroglyphic information, which divides at the epoch of Thothmes III. the Hebrews into two tribes, those of Jacob and Joseph, and of the Bible at the epoch of the Exodus, which gives us perfectly the same impression.

'Genesis finishes with the death of Jacob and of Joseph, and Exodus commences, so to say, with Moses. What had passed between these two epochs? It is then that the hieroglyphs show us two tribes. The one calling itself Jacob-el, the other Joseph-el, made prisoners by Thothmes III., at Magiddo, and brought captive into Egypt to Thebes. Have we here a lost page of the Bible?'

Professor Maspero objects that these lists are not of tribes or peoples, except in the case of such ethnic names as Rutennu, Kheta, &c., which figure at the beginning, 'as titles of a chapter, and not in the body of the chapter itself; Ioushep-ilou, Iakob-ilou, represent then, according to analogy, either compact villages or districts of small extent, forming what we still call in the East a *beled*, that is a number of houses or huts scattered in small groups, but belonging to one and the same chief or chiefs. But is this saying that the names are entirely unconnected with the two Hebrew patriarchs? The scribes who gathered the primitive history of Judæa found the narratives relating to Jacob and Joseph scattered over the territory, and must often have localized them in availing themselves of the assonances which certain geographical names presented with the names of the patriarchs. The town of Gerar and the Wâdy Gerar play a great part in the history of Abraham and of Isaac ; the localities Ioushep-ilou, Iakob-ilou may have been attached in the same way to the name of Jacob and to that of Joseph by some tradition now lost [1].'

In my communication to the Society of Biblical Archæology on the List of Palestine (May 3, 1887), I

[1] *Transactions of the Victoria Institute*, May 7, 1888.

have said : ' For 78 I have already suggested Yâsûf as a
" local habitation," and it seems to me possible that I'aqbāl
may be found in Khŭrbet Iqbâla [1]. The y̆ may have
been changed for *alif* [2] ; and, whether we regard the name
as personal or tribal, it is evident that it may have been
attached to a place, and found there by Thothmes, and
enrolled for tribute.

Iqbâla is six miles west of Jerusalem, a little way
south of the road to Jaffa, " at a spring in the valley," and
six miles south of Beit 'Ûr el Foka (Upper Beth-
Khoron).' A Wâdy Iqbâla runs northward from it.

I do not insist on this suggestion, or on that of
Yusepheh (Yâsûf) for the other name. Some other and
better explanation may be found. But it would be a
great omission in writing on the life and heritage of
Joseph to take no account of these interesting points.

M. Groff, in a later communication to the *Revue
Égyptologique* (1885, p. 151), thus writes : ' It is now many
years since that in reading attentively the sacred history
we were forcibly struck by the coincidence that Genesis
halts abruptly about the epoch when profane history
informs us that the Semitic Shepherd-kings were expelled
from Egypt. Tradition places the descent of Israel into
Egypt under the Shepherd-king Aphobis, and the first
Sallier papyrus tells us of a revolt of the Egyptians
against a king called Apapi.

' Exodus only takes up the history with Ramses II.
This enormous gap in the Hebrew text stretches then
since nearly the end (?) of the XVIIth dynasty to the

---

[1] Sheet xvii. Lt. ; *Name Lists*, p. 307 ; *Memoirs*, vol. iii. pp. 163, 165 ;
Quarterly Statement, 1884, pp. 184, 242 ; 1886, p. 57.

[2] See *Name Lists*, Introduction.

middle of the XIXth. We asked ourselves then if there were not among the hieroglyphic texts of Egypt something which might be likely to fill it. Our work is perhaps a first ray of light in these shades. We have established a fixed point round which other historic facts will group themselves. For where the Bible is silent the hieroglyphics speak.'

I cannot accept M. Groff's hypothesis that the families of Jacob and of Joseph had gone back at the expulsion of the Hyksôs rulers by Aahmes I., and had been found by Thothmes III. in Palestine, and brought back into Egypt among his prisoners of war. That their names had clung to their possessions, and had so been enrolled among other localities, appears likely enough. But it is not quite right to say that the Book of Exodus only takes up the history with Râmeses II. For the book, with its conjunctive first word, gives us the roll of names, and adds very much in a few words in continuation of the last words of Genesis: 'And Joseph died, and all his brethren, and all that generation. And the children of Israel were fruitful, and increased abundantly, and multiplied, and waxed exceeding mighty; and the land was filled with them.' And we find them where we had left them, in the eastward part of the Delta, with no hint of anything but continuance there during the interim.

With regard to the exact date of the Karnak tribute-lists of Thothmes III. we have now further information to go upon, for in the *Zeitschrift für Aegyptische Sprache*, Sept. 1889, is an elaborate and important article on the absolute dates of the reign of that great king, grounded on astronomical data and calculations, from which it is concluded that he came to the throne on the 20th March, in the year 1503, and died on the 14th February, in the year 1449 B.C. The author of this paper is Dr. Eduard Mahler, of Vienna; and from a note at the conclusion, by the celebrated editor of the journal, Brugsch-Pasha, it would appear that these results are assured.

Now we know that it was in the twenty-third year of the reign of Thothmes that the great campaign of Megiddo was achieved, and this will give us the year 1480 B.C.

The Exodus took place probably in the first quarter of the 13th century, so that our knowledge of all these names in Palestine dates from about two centuries before that great event. The entire and unquestioned sovereignty of all the countries between the Nile and the Euphrates, which we find established some eighty years later in the time of Amen-hotêp III., as proved by the correspondence from royal persons in Babylonia and Northern Syria, contained in the cuneiform tablets of Tel-el-Amarna, shows us how real and substantial the conquest of our Thothmes must have been, and how unquestioned his authority. It is true indeed that the seat of government and centre of military and civil splendour was Thebes in Upper Egypt; and so much the more, perhaps, were the pastoral and agricultural dwellers in Goshen undisturbed and prosperous.

We should notice that even in the darkest day of Israel's affliction the Egyptians with whom they were in daily and familiar contact seem to have been friendly enough; and it was only the unscrupulous tyranny

of the Pharaoh of a new dynasty (the XIXth) 'who
knew not Joseph,' and did not care for the honourable
conditions and antecedents of the Hebrew people, that
brought down all the sore load of slavery upon their
backs. But further on we shall take up the thread
of Egyptian history between the death of Joseph, and
the day when he was laid by his descendant Joshua
in the destined sepulchre at Shekem.

CHAPTER XI.

JACOB'S PROPHECY AND DEATH.

TO return now to the death-bed of Jacob. How instinctive and intense is the feeling of human continuity in the family, that noble sentiment which looks back with loyalty and reverence to 'our fathers' and 'the old time before them,' and is ever piously in earnest

'to bind
The generations each to each.'

In this sort the history of Joseph issued from the life of Jacob : 'These are the generations of Jacob : Joseph, being seventeen years old, was feeding the flock with his brethren.' And so now as to Jacob, 'he blessed *Joseph*, and said :

'The God before whom my fathers Abraham and Isaac did walk:
The God which hath fed me all my life unto this day ;
The Angel which hath redeemed me from all evil : bless *the lads !*'

How divinely taught is this patriarchal utterance, which reaches its highest mark in the sacred personal remembrance of the redeeming, rescuing Angel (המלאך הגאל), the Divine man of Penuel. Well says Franz

Delitzsch : ' Jacob's history, in spite of many shadows, is wonderfully guided by God's loving-kindness and truth.   His life makes the total impression that salvation is "not of works" (Rom. ix. 11), and it attains in Peniel as high a point as Abraham's on Moriah.   Not the blessing of the firstborn, secured from Esau by cunning, but that obtained from God by wrestling, becomes the basis of the nation which bears the name Israel, born of the labour of prayer and repentant tears (Hos. xii. 4) [1].'

We are not concerned in a life of Joseph to take into account the blessings pronounced by their father on the other sons of Israel, but only those on Joseph and his sons (Gen. xlix. 22–26).

Here the love and thankfulness of the patriarch spring up like a fountain, and overflow.   We follow the Revised Version :—

> ' Joseph is a fruitful bough,
> A fruitful bough by a fountain :
> His branches run over the wall.
> The archers have sorely grieved him,
> And shot at him, and persecuted him :
> But his bow abode in strength,
> And the arms of his hands were made strong,
> By the hands of the Mighty One of Jacob,
> (From thence is the Shepherd, the Stone of Israel,)
> Even by the God of thy father, who shall help thee,
> And by the Almighty, who shall bless thee,
> With blessings of heaven above,
> Blessings of the deep that coucheth beneath,
> Blessings of the breasts, and of the womb.
> The blessings of thy father
> Have prevailed above the blessings of my progenitors

[1] *Old Test. Hist. of Redemption*, trans. by S. I. Curtis; Clark, Edin., p. 50.

Unto the utmost bound of the everlasting hills:
They shall be on the head of Joseph,
And on the crown of the head of him that was separate from his brethren.'

I do not think the 'fruitful bough by a fountain' is simply a figure of one who should 'become a multitude,' but rather expresses the noble deeds and beneficent work of Joseph, which were spreading beyond the frontier wall of old Egypt, and would so widely bless the nations after the word of God had been fulfilled in planting His vine in His own destined vine-yard. We must remember that Joshua was himself a prince of Ephraim.

'But his bow abode in strength;'

not starting aside like a broken bow. The fine description of Joseph's defensive power in the days of persecution may well remind us of our great poet's words :

'Thrice is he armed who hath his quarrel just.'

The word אביר, 'Mighty' One, is only used of God in the connexion, 'Mighty One of Jacob,' or ' of Israel ; ' namely, in this passage, twice in Ps. cxxxii, and three times in the Book of Isaiah, i. 24; xlix. 26; lx. 16. From that Mighty One, says Jacob, ' is the Shepherd, the Stone of Israel.' Our minds naturally and rightly think of the Good Shepherd ; of the Stone which the builders rejected, but which became the Chief Corner-Stone.

Then follows the great benediction of Joseph's house in fruitfulness and blessings of the height above and the deep below, transcending all the ancestral blessings of time past : 'They shall be upon the head of Joseph, even on the crown of the head of him that was separate from his brethren :' separate (נזיר), consecrated for pre-eminence.

Now the venerable patriarch, blessed and blessing, does not pass away as on the wings of his inspired rapture, but gives his last directions in the most explicit and methodical way, with every business-like detail specified to the utmost—an example to all fathers. 'And he charged them, and said unto them, I am to be gathered unto my people : bury me with my fathers in the cave that is in the field of Ephron the Hittite, in the cave that is in the field of Makpelah, which is before Mamre, in the land of Canaan, which Abraham bought with the field from Ephron the Hittite for a possession of a burying-place : there they buried Abraham and Sarah his wife ; there they buried Isaac and Rebekah his wife; and there I buried Leah : the field and the cave that is therein, which was purchased from the children of Heth.'

Yes ! 'They are not to be heard which feign that the old fathers did look only for transitory promises.' It was in no such spirit, but 'by faith' that 'Jacob, when he was a-dying, blessed each of the sons of Joseph,' and, like Joseph afterwards, 'gave commandment concerning his bones.' It was that great faith that dignified with high significance those details of identification and title of the 'possession of a burial-place,' and the recital of names so venerated and so dear. 'And when Jacob made an end of charging his sons, he gathered up his feet into the bed, and yielded up the ghost, and was gathered unto his people.' Yes, he was gathered then and there, and went down to Sheol, not mourning for his son Joseph, but blessing him. 'And Joseph fell upon his father's face, and wept upon him, and kissed him : ' and doubtless first closed his eyes for their long sleep, as God had said.

' And Joseph commanded his servants the physicians to embalm his father : and the physicians embalmed Israel.'

Never among any people was the lore of the tomb so developed and refined as among the Egyptians.

The medical art was also very early brought to great advancement, and the medical papyri are of high interest to our own men of science. The physicians appear to have been from the first anxious to gain information from foreigners ; and the Ebers papyrus contains a receipt for eye-salve (most important in Egypt), procured from a Syrian of Gebal. The religious regard in which the bodies of the departed were held prevented the free dissection for the purposes of science. Dr. Ebers has touched skilfully this point in his life-like character of the student of Nature in *Uarda*. But the physicians were a branch of the great hierarchy, and the perpetual treatment necessary for embalming enabled them to ascertain better than any other race the characteristics of disorders on the basis of anatomy, and it was indeed enjoined by kings that their mortal diseases should be discovered, if possible, by such means.

The aromatics and asphalte so largely needed for embalming were imported from Palestine and Arabia, as we have seen, in the merchandise of those traders to whom Joseph himself had been sold as a slave, and afterwards in the gifts which his father, all unaware, had sent to his long-lost son by the hands of his brethren.

The word translated 'embalm' (חנט), is only used in Holy Scripture here, and in the Song of Solomon ii. 13, where it is applied to the ripening of figs.

The equivalent Arabic word 'has also,' says Lange, 'both these senses of ripening and embalming.'

It is possible that Joseph's own 'servants the physicians' may have dispensed with some of the Egyptian observances of a religious kind, and that they may be distinguished from the Egyptian priestly masters of the obsequies, and so (as the Abbé Vigouroux believes) by Joseph's pious care the observances of the Ritual were avoided.

Jacob had been moved by the desire to avoid lying in an Egyptian sepulchre, surrounded by the 'pomp and circumstance' of that religion which he repudiated, as Abraham had declined 'the choice' of the sepulchres of the sons of Kheth.

It may probably have been at Bubastis (Pi-beseth) that Jacob was embalmed, and the forty days spent in that elaborate service of spicing, and swathing, and coffining the venerated body, that it might be forthcoming at the great day; for the Egyptians believed, as Abraham did, 'that God is able to raise from the dead.' Was it likely that Jacob and his descendants would starve their souls in a creed less hopeful and exalting than that of the Egyptians, or the Chaldæans of Abram's fatherland?

'And forty days were fulfilled for him; for so are fulfilled the days of embalming.'

And then, it seems, the physicians restored the body to the family: 'and the Egyptians wept for him threescore and ten days.' Herodotus gives seventy days for the process of conservation. Diodorus says that upwards of thirty days are occupied in applying oil of cedar and other things to the whole body ; after which they add myrrh, cinnamon, and other drugs, which have not only the power of preserving the body for a length of time, but of imparting to it a fragrant odour. It is then restored to the friends of the deceased[1]. Diodorus also says that there was a general mourning for seventy-two days for the death of an Egyptian king.

It is to be observed that '*the Egyptians*' wept for the father of their viceroy seventy days. We are not told what the mourning of the Hebrews was on this occasion. When they lost their great deliverer and law-giver, 'the children of Israel wept for Moses in the plains of Moab thirty days: so the days of weeping and mourning for Moses were ended[2].' They had been expressly enjoined to put away all excessive and superstitious observances of the heathen at such times.

The Egyptians in all ages have been, if we may so say, wild and fanatical mourners. Even when 'the days of weeping for him [Jacob] were past,' Joseph, still a mourner, with his father unburied, could not, as on the old happy occasion, 'go in and tell Pharaoh' his desires ; but, according to the correct observance, he 'spake unto *the house* of Pharaoh [that is, to the officers of state], saying, If now I have found grace in your eyes, speak, I pray you, in the ears of Pharaoh, saying, My father made me swear, saying, Lo, I die ; in my grave which I have digged for me in the land of Canaan, there shalt thou bury me. Now, therefore, let

---

[1] Wilkinson, *The Ancient Egyptians*, edit. by Birch, vol. iii. p. 472.
[2] Deut. xxxiv. 8.

me go up, I pray thee, and bury my father, and I will come again.'

Joseph would not venture to speak to the Pharaoh in person, because the Hebrew custom of letting the hair and beard grow in mourning would exclude him from the presence-chamber of 'his holiness.' This is one of the very numerous and varied points which display the ' Ægypticity' of the narrative, to use the happy expression of Dr. Ebers.

And Pharaoh said, 'Go up, and bury thy father, according as he made thee swear.'

Doubtless what Jacob meant by 'my grave, which I have digged for me in the land of Canaan,' was the sepulchral recess (קבר) which he had hewn out of the rock within the cave of Makpelah.

We may notice that at this time there was no difficulty expected in going to Hebron and claiming access to the tomb where, as the last interment, Jacob had buried Leah.

It was the opinion of Mariette that the last Hyksôs dynasty belonged to the race of Kheta or Hittites. If that were so, the way would be clear indeed. At all events the sons of Kheth were at Hebron, as joint masters, with their intimate allies the Amorites, in Abraham's days, and the celebrated information as to the building (or re-building) of Zoan seven years later than Hebron[1], certainly seems, equally with the common devotion to the god Sutekh, to connect the Kheta with the domination of the Hyksôs in Lower Egypt. Set or Sutekh was fully identified in Egypt with Ba'al ; and it is interesting to find that the Phœnician Ba'al-worship was taught by Jezebel to Ahab, 'according to all (things) as did the Amorites[2].'

[1] Num. xiii. 22.   [2] 1 Kings xxi. 26.

Those who have studied the Egyptian data well know how thoroughly the Kheta were locked in and dovetailed, as it were, with the Amorites in the north and south alike, just as we find them in the Bible; and it seems in a high degree probable that both these strong races together were deeply involved in the Hyksôs invasion and lordship of Lower Egypt. They were fortress-builders and chariot-soldiers, and the nomad hordes of Shasu were their auxiliaries.

'And Joseph went up to bury his father: and with him went up all the servants of Pharaoh, the elders of his house, and all the elders of the land of Egypt, and all the house of Joseph, and his brethren, and his father's house: only their little ones, and their flocks, and their herds, they left in the land of Goshen. And there went up with him both chariots and horsemen: and it was a very great company.'

The way was open, and the great and princely pomp of the long funeral procession drew out its march through the fortified portals of the eastern wall of Egypt into the desert, having passed through the whole length of the green pasturage of Goshen.

The splendour of such processions is described and exhibited in the works of Rosellini, Wilkinson, and others. Long pilgrimages of mourning were often made for kings and great nobles in Egypt itself, and the sacred waters of the Nile became the highway. But such a progress across the sandy and stony expanses of the eastern desert must have been seldom seen. The route probably lay by the ancient way, re-discovered a few years since by the accomplished and lamented Rev. F. W. Holland, which leads due east from Ismaïlia. He

H

wrote to me in May, 1880 : ' The road which I discovered
. . . . will, I hope, have had a special interest for you,
as the route of Abraham into Egypt. It is a very
remarkable road, evidently much used in ancient times,
and it is curious that it has remained unknown.' Professor
Maspero agrees with me in thinking that this was the
route by which Seti I., the father of the Pharaoh of the
long oppression, led up his troops to the attack of the
fortress of Kanāna, which would certainly appear, as
Major Conder says, to be the site marked at this day
by the name of Khŭrbet-Kan'ân, the ruin of Kan'ân
(Hebrew, כנען).

'The ruin occupies a knoll in a very important position on high ground, the two main roads to Hebron, one
from Gaza, by Dura (Adoraim), one from Beer-sheba, on
the south [this was Seti's route], join close to the knoll
of Khŭrbet-Kan'ân, and run thence, north-west, about one
and a half mile to Hebron. West of the ruin is 'Ain-el-
Unkŭr . . . . which issues from the rock, and gives a
fine perennial supply, forming a stream even in autumn.'
I do not doubt that they halted at the hallowed camping-
place and wells of Beer-sheba.

' And they came to the threshing-floor of Atad, which
is beyond Jordan, and there they lamented with a very
great and sore lamentation : and he made a mourning
for his father seven days.'

A notion has arisen that the route of the great funeral
procession lay to the east of the Dead Sea, through the
land of Moab, and across the Jordan at the ford now so
celebrated, and so over the mountain country southward
to Hebron. The only ground for this appears to be the
identification of the threshing-floor of Atad, by Jerome

in his *Onomasticon* with Beth Hoglah, which is itself
identified with 'Ain Hajlah, a little way to the west
of the Jordan, above the Dead Sea. Dr. Thomson
says : 'There was another Bethagla in the land of the
Philistines ;' and it seems very unlikely that such a route
should have been taken ; and we agree with Bishop
Wordsworth and Dr. Thomson, and with Kalisch, who
writes : 'The funeral procession seems to have taken
its way from the province of Goshen in a north-easterly
direction, . . . a journey from eight to ten days ; within
the boundaries of the land of Canaan, and, probably,
not much to the south of Hebron, it stopped "at the
threshing-floor of Atad," where both the sons of Jacob,
and the Egyptians who accompanied them, renewed
their mourning during seven days.'

The place of the mourning has not yet been identified,
and this is not a matter of surprise. The expression
'beyond the Jordan,' in connexion with the Canaanite
inhabitants, must certainly mean on the westward side,
and this would indicate the early date of the narrative,
written before the Israelites had taken possession. The
seven days' mourning which Joseph commanded was the
custom of the Hebrews, and the Egyptian retinue
observed it with them. The scene must have been very
impressive to the Canaanites who looked on that
unwonted spectacle ; and they were so struck by what
they saw and heard, that they called the level platform
of high ground where the assembly was gathered, Abel-
Mizraim, which might mean either the meadow or the
mourning of Egypt ; but, considering the position, which
was not a grassy irrigated place, but a high, exposed, and
windy platform, it seems that the Septuagint version and

the Vulgate give us the right translation, 'the mourning of Egypt.'

It is certainly an interesting coincidence, in view of the expression, 'the Canaanites saw the mourning' . . . . 'for his sons carried him into the land of Canaan,' that the fortified outpost of the great centre Hebron should be called the Ruin of Canaan, as we have seen, and that we can trace the name back to the fortress of Kanāna at an earlier time than the Exodus. Was the name Cana'an especially applied to the district of Hebron ? In the curious Arabic History of Jerusalem and Hebron of Mûjîr-ed-dîn (about A. D. 1500), he says it is reported that Solomon was bidden by God to build an enclosure above the tomb of Abraham ; and that, in consequence, he left Jerusalem, and went 'towards the land of Kana'an. After having turned in different directions without discovering the tomb, he returned to Jerusalem,' where he was told that a light from heaven would show him the tomb. This happened accordingly. This would agree with a local application of the name Cana'an [1].

In the account of the burial of Sarah it is especially said that Kiriath Arba' 'is Khebrôn in the land of Kana'an [2].'

It appears that the great escort and retinue of the Egyptians remained at the place of mourning whilst 'his sons did to him [Jacob] as he had commanded them : for his sons carried him *into the land of Canaan*, and buried him in the cave of the field of Makpelah, which Abraham bought with the field, for a possession of a burying-place, of Ephron the Hittite, before Mamre.'

---

[1] *Histoire de Jérusalem et d'Hébron, &c.*, trad. par Henri Sauvaire. Paris : Leroux, 1876, p. 13.   [2] Gen. xxiii. 2.

It was seventeen years since the patriarch had been so honourably brought down into Egypt, and now his soul had been gathered to his fathers in peace, and all those things that had seemed 'against him' in the hour of his bitter perplexity had wrought together for good, by God's blessing, under the hand of his lost son ; and his body had retraced the long road of pilgrimage to the sepulchre that he had hewn.

Hebron was a great sanctuary-city in the midst of the most fruitful valleys and terraced hill-sides. About A.D. 1000, Mukaddasi, an accomplished Arab traveller, thus describes Habrâ (Hebron) : 'All the country round Hebron, for the distance of half a stage, is filled with villages and vineyards, and grounds bearing grapes and apples, and it is even as though it were all but a single orchard of vines and fruit-trees. The district goes by the name of Jebel Nusrah[1]. Its equal for beauty does not exist elsewhere, nor can any fruits be finer. A great part of them are sent away to Egypt and into all the country round[2].'

Four centuries and a half earlier Antoninus Martyr visited the sanctuary, and found Christians and Jews worshipping separately, and he says :—'The burial of Jacob in that place is celebrated with great devotion by all on the first day after Christmas ; so that from all the land of the Jews an innumerable multitude collect together, bearing incense or lights, and bestowing gifts

---

[1] Wady, and Bîr, and Khŭrbet Nŭsâra are still found a little to the north of Hebron (*Memoirs*, vol. iii. detailed map of Hebron and its vicinity).

[2] *Description of Syria, &c.*, by Mukaddasi, translated by Guy le Strange. Pilgrims' Text Society, 1886, p. 51.

upon those who minister in the church[1].' With such devout memory was the burial of Jacob observed some two thousand two hundred years after his death.

At the last royal visit, July 28, 1881, Capt. (now Major) Conder, R.E., drew up a very careful memorandum, from which it seems, as we might expect, that the cave is artificially formed in the rock, and 'probably resembles many of the rock-cut sepulchres of Palestine, with a square ante-chamber carefully quarried, and two interior sepulchral chambers, to which access has been made at a later period through the roofs. It is, however, possible that the ante-chamber may be a later addition, and partly built of masonry[2].' 'The shrines of Isaac and Rebekah are the only two which seem probably to stand over the actual caves, and Jelâl-ed-Dîn says that Jacob was buried "before the entrance to the sepulchral cave," which agrees with the present position of his cenotaph, and with what has been already said as to the probable extent of the cave.'

Hebron is a most venerable city.   Mr. Flinders Petrie, in speaking of Zoan, observes : 'This coupling of it with a Palestinian city[3] shows that the building must refer to a settlement by Shemites, and not by Egyptians; and, considering the age of Hebron, it probably refers to the settlement before the XIth dynasty.'

In my *Studies on the Times of Abraham*, I have discussed the origin of Hebron, which was at first built by the Anakim, who called it Kiriath-Arba', after the name of Arba', the father of Anak. I have suggested that Arba', which means Four, may stand as the numerical

---

[1] *Antoninus Martyr*, Pal. P. Text Soc. 1885, p. 24.
[2] *Pal. Exp. F. Memoirs*, vol. iii. p. 338.   [3] Hebron, Num. xiii. 22.

symbol of a god, according to the system of the Chaldæans, either a deified hero, or a god regarded as a race-
father in the olden fashion.

This may be the more likely, since Arba' was claimed
as the Father of the Libyans, as Pleyte has shown,
quoting Movers. This would agree well with the ancient
belief that the Canaanites were, to a great extent, driven
far westward into North Africa [1].

From the Biblical evidence I formed the opinion that
the Anakim were probably the ruling race of the Amorites, and I have elsewhere given reasons for the supposition that the fair and blue-eyed Libyans were of the
same stock.

Mr. Petrie describes the Amorites depicted as defend-
ing the fort of Amâr in the celebrated Egyptian tableau
as having 'the skin light red, rather pinker than flesh
colour.' Osburn writes: ' The personal appearance of the
Amorites resembles a good deal that of the Zuzim [a
mistake for Shasu]; the complexion is sallow, the eyes
blue, the eyebrows and beards red, the hair so much
darker, from exposure or other causes, as to be painted
black. The features were regular, the nose perhaps
scarcely so prominent as among the Zuzim' [Shasu].

The Amorites came, I have always believed, from the
plain of the Euphrates, whatever their original seat, and
Professor Sayce has well pointed to Beth-ammaris, and
Ap-ammeris, west of the Euphrates, as preserving their
name, which has a chief halting-place at Gar-emeri-s,
the region of Damascus.

A tribe of them were called Yebûsi (Jebusites), and had
their stronghold where David drove them out, or at least

---

[1] *Religion des Pré-israélites*, pp. 63, 212.

put them down ; and here, as elsewhere, they were dovetailed with the Hittite in a very remarkable way.   This
was true at Hebron, Yebûs, Tabor, Megiddo, Kadesh on
the Orontes ; and doubtless these are merely examples ;
and this fact is as clear in the Bible as out of it.   The
Gibeonites were also Amorites [1], and Khivvites.   Mr.
Petrie, in his valuable series of casts, now in the
British Museum, has given us a good series of Amorites
of different dates, but all of the same type, showing a
handsome and regular profile of sub-aquiline cast, the
nose continuing the line of the sloping forehead.   The
cheek-bones are high, the faces have a decided and mar-
tial expression, and look like those of tall, strong men, as
we know them to have been.   They wear long robes
and capes, like most Syrians of those times.

In a most interesting article in *The Expositor* [2], Professor Sayce has described ' *The white race of ancient
Palestine,*' comparing their physical character, as shown
in the Egyptian wall-paintings, with those of the Kabyles
of Northern Africa and the fair people of Palestine.   ' If
there is still a white race in Palestine,' he writes, ' it is
because there was a white race there before the days of
the Exodus.'

' The united testimony of the Old Testament and the
Egyptian monuments shows that this race was known by
the name of Amorite, and, like the Kabyles of Africa,
inhabited the mountainous regions (Num. xiii. 29 ; Deut.
i. 20).   It was the aboriginal race which had been destroyed before the Israelites, though their " height was
like the height of the cedars " (Amos ii. 9).   In the neighbourhood of the old sacred city of Hebron they were

---

[1] 2 Sam. xxi. 2.   [2] Vol. viii.

known as the sons of Anak (Deut. i. 27, 28 ; so Josh. xi.
21, 22, compared with x. 5, 38).'

I must not continue the interesting quotation, but refer
to the article.

At Hebron the names of the Amorite princes Eshkol
and Mamre were geographically fixed, and it is quite
clear that they must have been as closely united with
the Hittites, Ephron and the rest, as they were at the
Amorite city of Yebûs, of which the Prophet Ezekiel
tells us that its mother was a Hittite and its father an
Amorite [1].

We must people these terraced mountain-sides and
these watered and fruitful valleys with the tall, fair, and
strong Amorites and their lordly allies, and indeed
masters, the sallow, black-haired Hittites, in this southern
outpost of their united settlements, when the splendid
array of Egypt escorted the Hebrew procession of
mourners to the border of Canaan on their way to the
purchased possession of a burying-place ' in the cave that
is in the field of Makpelah before Mamre.'

The alliance, which had perhaps given the name Khebron to the city, and had been confirmed by a covenant,
by the joint expedition of Abraham's house and the
Amorite warriors against Kedor-la'omer, and by the
purchase of the field and cave, was held unbroken and in
honour.

We may reasonably ask the question : Was the possession in any way enclosed or protected at that time?

The stately and ancient enclosure-wall now standing,
is considered by the highest authorities to be Herodian
work, and contemporary with precisely similar work, with

[1] Ezek. xvi. 3, 45.

the same flat, shallow pilaster-buttresses, at Jerusalem.
Sir C. W. Wilson, K.C.B., R.E., writes: 'Both at
Jerusalem and Hebron a level platform is obtained by
massive walls of large stones, with marginal drafts.   At
Hebron a surrounding wall, ornamented with pilasters,
rises to a height of twenty-five feet above the platform,
and it is probable that Herod's temple enclosure was
surrounded by a similar wall, which has long since dis-
appeared, with the exception of a solitary fragment which
was discovered by Captain Conder a few years ago.   It
would almost seem as if the Hebron Haram were a copy
in miniature of the Temple enclosure at Jerusalem[1].'

Major Conder had written (p. 342): 'There is no
reason to believe that any building was erected on the
spot before the Captivity.'   This opinion is, of course,
quite contrary to the well-known argument of the late
Dean Stanley, who takes the expression of Josephus:
μνημεῖα . . . . καλῆς μαρμάρου καὶ φιλοτίμης εἰργασμένα[2],
as applying to the present structure, and writes: 'Josephus, in his *Antiquities*, tells us that there were "monuments built there by Abraham and his descendants;"
["both Abraham and his descendants built themselves
sepulchres in that place[3],"] and in his *Jewish War*, that
"the monuments of Abraham and his sons" (apparently
alluding to those already mentioned in the *Antiquities*)
"were still shown at Hebron, of beautiful marble, and
admirably worked."'

'These monuments can hardly be other than what the
"Bordeaux Pilgrim," in A. D. 333, describes as "a quad-
rangle of stones of astonishing beauty;" and these

---

[1] *Memoirs*, vol. iii. p. 346.   [2] *Bell. Jud.* iv., ix. 7.
[3] *Ant.* I., xiv.

again are clearly those which exist at the present day—
the massive enclosure of the mosque.   For the walls,
as they now stand, and as Josephus speaks of them,
must have been built before his time.   The terms which
he uses imply this; and he omits to mention them
amongst the works of Herod the Great, the only potentate who could or would have built them in his time, and
amongst whose buildings they must have occupied, if at
all, a distinguished place.

'But, if not erected by Herod, there is then no period
at which we can stop short of the monarchy.   So
elaborate and costly a structure is inconceivable in the
disturbed and impoverished state of the nation after the
Return.   It is to the kings, at least, that the walls must
be referred, and, if so, to none so likely as one of the
sovereigns to whom they are ascribed by Jewish and
Mussulman tradition, David or Solomon.   Beyond this
we can hardly expect to find a continuous proof.   But,
by this time, we have almost joined the earlier tradition
implied in the reception of the Book of Genesis, with its
detailed local description, into the Jewish Sacred Books[1].'

Such is the argument of Stanley.   For my own part, I
cannot think that the μνημεῖα of Josephus can be the
present structure.

But, apart from the date of the existing enclosure-
walls, there are certain considerations which have struck
me with great force in regard to the matter, but which
have, I believe, never been brought forward.   The two
points are these.   First, the orientation of the enclosure.
The oblong structure does not conform in its emplacement to the natural fall of the hill-side, but strongly

[1] *History of the Jewish Church*, ed. 1883, vol. i. p. 432.

violates it for the sake of obtaining that position, with the angles toward the cardinal points, which characterizes the ancient sacred places of early Chaldæa, not of Egypt, nor of the Temple-enclosure of Jerusalem. This seems to me to suggest the likelihood that the builder of the present structure may have followed the lines of some more ancient defensive or enclosing work laid out on the Chaldæan plan, and after the manner of the temple of the Moon-god at Ur of the Chaldees, the familiar sanctuary of Abraham's youth, whose ruins still remain at Mugheir[1]. Sir C. W. Wilson kindly gave me a memorandum and drawing of the Hebron Haram many years ago. From the former I quote : 'The building is on the side of a hill which has been partly excavated to receive the foundations ; the plinth course, which is on the ground-level in rear, has in front from five to seven courses beneath it, seven at the S.W. angle, five at N.E. angle.'

Thus we see that it was considered indispensable to make the angles face the cardinal points, even at the expense of an awkward irregularity as regards the slope of the ground, for the building is thrust into the hill-side in an angular fashion. It is interesting, by the way, to notice that the boundary-stones of Gezer (Tell Jazer) mark out a quadrangular space of land with the corners bearing towards the cardinal points. Neither the ancient and interesting walled enclosure known as the House of Abraham (Beit-el-Khŭlîl), near Hebron, nor the Temple site at Jerusalem, have the same bearings, but are faced with their sides to the cardinal points.

Secondly, the next remarkable point of comparison

---

[1] *Studies on the Times of Abraham*, p. 12, and plate II.

with Chaldæan structures is found in the mode of building with shallow pilaster-buttresses. This is the exact
mode adopted in the earliest buildings of Southern
Chaldæa, and followed also in examples of Assyrian
masonry. A very good early example may be found in
the lowest and oldest portion of the great temple of
Mugheir, and another in the great enclosure called
Wuswas at Warka (the ancient Erech), faced like the
temple of Mugheir in its orientation.

The original drawings of Mr. Churchill, the artist who
accompanied Mr. Loftus, are in the British Museum,
and one of these [1] shows the construction of the brick-
work with square pilasters as at Hebron, the breadth
of the interspaces being twice that of the pilasters,
which is not materially different from the proportion
at Hebron.

The same style, carried out more elaborately, is
characteristic of Chaldæan and of Assyrian work, and
also curiously characteristic of early Egyptian ornamentation.

Now I cannot at all agree with Fergusson that 'the
cave seems to have been left open, protected only by its
own sanctity, like so many other sepulchres in Judea,
till about the Christian era.' It seems to me far more
likely that Abraham would have taken advantage of
what had been familiar to him in Chaldæa, and of what
he had seen in Egypt. In Chaldæa, it is true, there
were no caves in rocky hill-sides, but the preservation of
the dead was most carefully and elaborately considered ;
and in Egypt, where sunken excavations were the rule,

---

[1] Badly shown in a wood-cut in Loftus's *Chaldæa*, p. 172.

the entrances were guarded by strong and elaborate structures above ground[1].

The sepulchral chamber was an underground cave, or system of such, and above ground was an oblong raised structure, of which the successive courses were a little set back, so as to produce a battering or sloping face; this structure enclosed a chamber for funeral observances above ground, and protected the entrances to the subterranean tombs. Such was the general character of the sepulchres of the old empire in the neighbourhood of Memphis. And the ornamentation of those parts within and at the entrances which were not left plain was of the same style, which we call perpendicular panelling, as that of the Chaldæan brick buildings. This has also struck M. Perrot, who writes: 'The Egyptian architect had recourse to the same motive, first, in the tombs of the ancient empire for the decoration of the chamber walls in the mastabas; secondly, for the relief of great brick surfaces. The resemblance to the Mesopotamian work is sometimes very great[2].'

It is a curious coincidence that the exterior cornice surmounting the walls at Hebron consists simply of flat projecting slabs squared at the edges, well shown in de Vogüé's plate[3].

But exactly a similar finishing of walls at the top is shown in Assyrian reliefs in fortified towns besieged by that nation, as for instance in Rawlinson's *Ancient*

[1] The *Mastabas* of the more ancient times have been described by Mariette (*Revue Archéologique*, 1869), and in the fine work of Perrot and Chipiez on Egyptian art (page 169, &c., French edition), and by Maspero in his excellent condensed work *L'Archéologie Égyptienne*, p. 109, &c.

[2] *Art in Chaldæa*, &c., Eng. trans., vol. i. p. 248.

[3] *Temple de Jérusalem*, p. 119.

Monarchies, vol. i. p. 469; in *Art in Chaldæa*, by Perrot and Chipiez, vol. ii. p. 74. It is also worthy of remark that the length of the oldest and lowest stage of the temple of the Moon-god at Ur (Mugheir) is given as 198 feet, and that of the enclosure at Hebron by Major Conder as 197 feet, but by Fergusson as 198 feet.

Now my suggestion is this : that perhaps the existing structure replaced the ruins of one far more ancient, and dating originally from the time of.Abraham ; intended to enclose and cover and guard the possession of a burial-place for the heads of his race.

We may well imagine that Egyptian, or Phœnician, or even Hittite craftsmen might well enough have built what Abraham required ; and let us recollect that the fortresses of the Anakim and Hittites are represented on the walls of Karnak and Luqsor as lofty and formidable enough, ' great and walled up to heaven.'

Some such structure would have given defence to David during the early part of his reign, when Hebron was his capital.

At all events it seems to me that Abraham, whom the Hittites recognized as 'a prince of God,' would be far more likely to secure his sepulchre in the best and most costly and perfect way known to him in his long and varied experience, than that it should have been 'left open, protected only by its own sanctity.' And if so, surely the peculiarities of emplacement, dimensions, and architectural character might well have been as far as possible imitated, and so preserved.

CHAPTER XII.

THE RETURN, AND AFFAIRS IN EGYPT.

THE next statement in the Biblical narrative is a very important one: 'And Joseph returned into Egypt, he, and his brethren, and all that went up with him to bury his father, after he had buried his father.'

So we know that none of all the house and dependants of Jacob and Joseph took the opportunity of this journey to remain behind in the land of Canaan.

This helps to strengthen the opinion that if we meet with the names Jacob-el and Joseph-el there some two centuries later, those names belong to localities, and not to their inhabitants as ancestral names at that time; but we will by and by compare some other statements of Holy Scripture.

And now a great misgiving seized the minds of Joseph's brethren, ' when they saw that their father was dead '—when, as we say, they realized it in earnest, and felt the great vacancy where he had been [1].

[1] 'They said [literally]. If Joseph hated us: — if returning he caused to return upon us all the evil which we did unto him— !' (Dr. Whitelaw in *The Pulpit Commentary*.)

This reminds us of the vindictive purpose of Esau in the prospect of his father's death, and the dread which made Rebekah warn Jacob to flee away to Laban for refuge.   But Joseph was not an Esau, and when the message came, reciting the old father's command for forgiveness, and the humble prayer of the penitents after seventeen years of security and bounty, we cannot wonder that Joseph wept to think of such misunderstanding, and most of all to hear this needless injunction from the grave.   And, when the messengers brought word of this, 'his brethren also went and fell down before his face; and they said, Behold, we be thy servants.'   So in that great parable the returning prodigal says: 'I am no more worthy to be called thy son: make me as one of thy hired servants.'   But Joseph once more reassures them in the same magnanimous and godly spirit as before: 'Fear not, for am I in the place of God? And as for you, ye meant evil against me; but God meant it for good, to bring to pass, as it is this day, to save much people alive.   Now therefore fear ye not: I will nourish you and your little ones.   And he comforted them, and spake to their hearts.'

Very well does Lange comment on this, that what Joseph says gives us the grand golden key to his whole life's history.   Bishop Wordsworth would take Joseph's words: 'for am I in the place of God?' as an assertion, 'I am in the place of God:' the sense seems to be (says the good bishop), 'Fear not, for I am a minister of God to you for good.   I was sent hither by the God of your fathers, who is a merciful God, to preserve life[1], and therefore you need not fear.'   This is confirmed

---

[1] See Gen. xlv. 5.

I

by the LXX version, and by what follows, and by the
Syriac and Arabic versions, which have: '*I fear God.*'

In such words: 'to preserve life,' 'I will nourish
you,' there seems an echo of Joseph's Egyptian title, if
that indeed means 'nourisher of the land.'

And with such divine glad tidings for the stricken
conscience Joseph 'evangelized' his brethren.   And the
next words carry us over a lapse of fifty-six years:
'And Joseph dwelt in Egypt, he, and his father's house:
and Joseph lived an hundred and ten years.'

It would be most interesting to know what historic
events filled up these fifty-six years.

We are indeed informed in an imperfect way from
Egyptian sources of the main outlines of that memorable
counter-revolution which drove out the foreign lords,
and enthroned in power the great XVIIIth dynasty in the
person of its founder Aahmes.

There were in succession at Thebes three princes who
bore the common name of Sekenen-Râ (Râ the war-like),
and the first of these, a simple prince, we find assuming
Pharaonic titles, although not the full style of a 'lord of
Upper and Lower Egypt.' This seems to show the
beginning of that patriotic struggle of which we see a
little here and there, and know the upshot.

This first Sekenen-Râ was called 'the Great;' his
successor the 'very Great;' and the third was called
the 'very Victorious' (Ta-āa-ken), who received divine
honours in later time.   As to him we happily know something; for two men of his time have left sepulchral inscriptions of great importance: both were called Aahmes
(son of the Moon-god), and one of them was the
admiral, son of Abana-Baba.   The sculptured likeness

of this brave sailor is thus described by Mr. Villiers Stuart : 'A bluff, resolute-looking man, more European than Egyptian in features, and not handsome. A short and rather snub nose, a low solid brow, and, what is most unusual with Egyptians, wearing his own hair, and whiskers on his lower jaw, and wearing also a short beard, curling upwards from his chin, after the manner of mariners any day to be seen at Portsmouth[1].'

This brave sailor received his first commission from the 'very Victorious,' in whose service his father was a captain ; for the prince had built a flotilla to go down the Nile and attack the Hyksôs in their stronghold in the Delta.

The war of liberation was drawing towards a successful issue when this valiant king ended his life in battle, and was dragged dead from the strife by his faithful soldiers, and embalmed in haste. His mummy lies, as we have said, in the Museum of Bûlaq[2], now removed to Gizeh.

The successor of the dead victor was Ka-mes, to whose queen Aah-hotep belonged that most interesting array of jewels found in her coffin which delighted the visitors to the Great Exhibition of 1862 in London, where they were deposited by Mariette from the Egyptian Museum. This honoured queen seems to have survived her husband, and to have been buried with profuse filial piety by her son Aahmes. This king is a potentate of the first rank. Emerging from the long struggle of the XVIIth Theban dynasty, it was he who besieged the great entrenched camp of the Hyksôs at Hauar (Avaris), and drove those

---

[1] *Nile Gleanings*, p. 234.

[2] These most interesting inscriptions are given in English in the *Records of the Past*, the first in vol. iv, and the latter in vol. vi.

alien lords quite out of the field of Zoan and all Lower
Egypt, and pursued them to Sharuhen, near Beersheba,
and ultimately defeated them there.

He also was found among the royal dead at Deir-el-
Bahri, surrounded by garlands of flowers in his coffin of
gold and blue, and on his breast his Pharaonic titles and
the figure of the great god Amen-Râ.

Now the record of the famine before mentioned refers
to the life-time of Abana-Baba, the father of the Admiral
Aahmes, if Brugsch is right; and in that case Joseph
would have been contemporary with the very valiant
Sekenen-Râ, and the warfare would have been going on
in his time.

But, as M. Naville has said, Joseph 'was a purely civil
dignitary; he does not seem to have had anything to
do with the military caste.'   And, although there seems
no guidance in the Scripture narrative which would lead
us to think of war in his days, yet conclusions from
mere absence of evidence are proverbially precarious;
and we cannot prove that these last fifty-six years of his
lifetime were spent without conflict, which to the court
in Lower Egypt would be accounted as insurrection of a
stubborn vassal.

At all events it seems clear enough that Joseph
anticipated no waning of his own prosperity when he
promised his brethren, on the loss of their father: ' I will
nourish you and your little ones.'

But next we come to the end of that half-century of
brotherly kindness and protection, during which ' Joseph
dwelt in Egypt, he, and his father's house. . . . And
Joseph saw Ephraim's children of the third generation'
(that is, Ephraim's great-grandchildren); ' the children

also of Machir, the son of Manasseh, were brought up upon Joseph's knees.'—the prosperous family of Ephraim, of whom arose Joshua, to fulfil his great ancestor's injunction ;—the house of Gilead, who mightily prevailed on the east of Jordan against the Amorites, and from whom sprung the valiant Jephthakh.   It is not wonderful that the continued presence, authority, counsel, and influence of Joseph for four generations should have enlightened and strengthened the two houses that bore his name, and have strongly cast their future in the fulfilment of their destined lot.

What is told us of Joseph's end upon earth is in great contrast to the full and elaborate account of the departure of his father: nothing can be more simple and quiet than the last words of Joseph, which, as far as they are recorded, only concern those that should come after him. ' And Joseph said unto his brethren, I die : but God will surely visit you [or remember you] and bring you up out of this land unto the land which He sware to Abraham, to Isaac, and to Jacob.'   And Joseph moreover solemnly repeats this assurance, and exacts a sacred promise, as his father had done of him : ' And Joseph took an oath of the children of Israel, saying, God will surely visit you, and ye shall carry up my bones from hence.

' So Joseph died, being an hundred and ten years old : and they embalmed him, and he was put in a coffin in Egypt.'   ' By faith Joseph, when his end was nigh, made mention of the departure of the children of Israel ; and gave commandment concerning his bones.'

So did the last end of Joseph agree with the whole of his life's work.   We have no hint of self-seeking or ambition of any kind, however honourable, or useful, or reputable, from first to last.

His afflictions came upon him undeserved, his honours unsought: being faithful in a little, God made him ruler over many cities, and wielder for good of the greatest power then upon earth.

It has been naturally asked by Kalisch, ' But why did not Joseph, like Jacob, order his remains to be forthwith conveyed to Canaan?' It is a very pertinent and suggestive question, which we cannot at present decisively answer.

But, in the light of such knowledge as we yet have with regard to the affairs of Egypt, it seems to me accounted for perhaps by the altered and more retired position of Joseph under a later Pharaoh than his old patron; perhaps by the troubles of internal war, which we have already sketched in outline, and the consequent disturbance of relations across the eastern frontier. And we seem to read between the lines in the expression, ' God will surely remember you, and bring you out of this land,' not only the spirit of the stranger and sojourner, loyal to the covenant, and sighing for the Promised Land, but also some fore-shadowing at least of that eclipse that should come upon them in a land that was not theirs.

' Joseph died, a son of one hundred and ten years;' and it is recorded of his great descendant Joshua, that he also had attained that age. Berosus gives a hundred and sixteen years as the ideal length of life among the Chaldæans. But among the Egyptians a hundred and ten years was for ages the desired limit.

As instances we may take one of a very early date; another, a little later than the Exodus, of the XIXth dynasty. The venerable Ptah-hotep, the oldest of known moralists, who lived in the ancient time of the Vth dynasty, says, 'I have passed a hundred and ten years of life by the gift of the king.' And in a court poem addressed to Seti II., the scribe assures him 'thou shalt dwell a hundred and ten years on the earth.' As Pierret writes: 'It is the number of years invariably adopted by the formulary of the inscriptions, whenever there is asked of the gods the boon of a long and happy existence.' Joseph had reached this milestone in his pilgrimage so much desired by the sons of Mizraim.

It is duly noticed that Joseph was embalmed and put in a coffin in Egypt, thus recording the ceremonial preservation of his body; and this was done in view of his last injunction. Doubtless this coffin was a wooden sepulchral chest (Hebrew אָרוֹן), such as the Egyptians often used to enclose their mummies.

We are not told that Joseph instructed the sons of Israel as to his chosen burial-place in the Promised Land. It is probable that, with characteristic thoughtfulness, he made no mention of this in the oath that he exacted from them, leaving the matter to be decided by the chiefs of his house and the leaders of his people when the appointed time should come.

The deposit of the mummy was a most sacred family trust; an object of great veneration and care, for which the Egyptians, more than any other people upon earth, made the most costly, self-denying, and elaborate provision.

Doubtless the charge devolved on Ephraim and his house; and Joshua would be in his generation the right guardian of the body of his great forefather.

CHAPTER XIII.

EGYPT TILL THE EXODUS.

WE do not feel that we have said farewell to Joseph, although indeed his life is over, until we have seen his bones carried across the Jordan in their stately receptacle, and safely deposited in his own inheritance. We will therefore endeavour to sketch the intermediate history in the light of the more recent results of Egyptological discovery.

We have already brought down the course of events to the expulsion of the Hyksôs with their military power out of Egypt. The great fortified position of Hauar, somewhere to the east of Zoan, has not yet been definitely identified. The Israelites in their pacific pursuits may not have been involved, at least in any large and corporate manner, in this war; and it is considered certain that other kindreds of foreign stocks were not expelled, but remain to this day, as Mariette has so graphically told us, in the marsh lands and wide expanse eastward of the main Nile-branches of the Delta.

Aahmes the conqueror, after he had pacified Egypt,

and secured his eastern line of defences, reopened the great white limestone quarries of Tûra, in the twenty-second year of his reign, near the present Cairo, for the structures of the temples of Memphis and Thebes. But the great scarcity of monumental or other relics of this whole XVIIIth dynasty in the Delta generally seems to show that the Pharaohs of that time avoided this part of the country as regards residence and their royal presence, and left it to the government of deputies. It was not till a later time that the land of Goshen was fully attended to, and brought into the regular system of Egyptian culture and administration.

Meanwhile the kings of Egypt, now equipped with the important chariot-forces, pushed across the frontier their conquests in Asia. Amenhotep I., and his son Thothmes I., undertook in earnest the conquest of Syria and Mesopotamia, and returned in triumph to Thebes with the spoils and captives of their wars. Next in the genealogy and on the throne came Thothmes II., and his ambitious and accomplished sister Hatasu (or Hatshepsu). This great lady, a high and mighty prince indeed, like our Queen Elizabeth, assumed the masculine symbols of Pharaonic dignity, and ruled with great intelligence and success. The expedition of her fleet down the Red Sea to the incense-bearing land of Pûn is graphically set forth in the beautiful relief-sculptures of her magnificent edifice of Deir-el-Bahri.

In her time all went well, and tribute came in freely ; but no sooner was this great queen's younger brother Thothmes III. left alone on the throne than a general rising broke out from the borders of Egypt to the northern frontier, and a muster of Asiatic enemies in great force took place at Megiddo, which led to the wars of this most distinguished of all the Pharaohs. A monument of high interest for his time is the inscription of Amen-em-heb, another hero of the mettle of Admiral Aahmes, who closely attended the person of the king in the Negeb of Southern Palestine, and all the way northwards to Naharina, on the Euphrates, fighting near Aleppo, at Karkemish, and in the land of Sentsar, and again at Kadesh on Orontes ; and another time at Nii, where the king killed 120 elephants for their ivory. Afterwards he attended Amenhotep II., the son and successor of Thothmes III., in his victorious campaigns. We find the prisoners taken in Naharina called by the familiar name of 'Amu, which reminds us that Balaam is described as dwelling by the river (Euphrates) in the land of the Benê-'Amu. He was a lord of the 'Amu, the Semites, in close contact with the Khatti or Kheta[1].

The vast and successful enterprises of this great king are very well summed up by Brugsch in his history—I quote from the English translation :—' Henceforward an important field is opened to our enquiries. Egypt itself forms the central point of a world-intercourse, which, carried on by trade and war, affords us an unexpected view into the past, and into the life of the peoples of this very old period of the world. We shall see how the king undertook to measure himself in battle with the mightiest empire of the old time, and how he carried his

---

[1] It is a striking illustration of the collocation of separate races that the Egyptian tableaux represent two highly-contrasted types under the name Ruten, or Luten, the one thoroughly Semitic, the other quite resembling the Kheta. This may be well seen in Mr. Petrie's collection of casts of ethnic types in the British Museum, to which we have before referred.

arms to the extremest frontiers of the then known earth, whether it were in Asia towards the east, or in Libya towards the west, or in the south as far as the heart of Africa. We shall learn by name and number, by quantity and weight, a complete list of the productions of foreign countries ; some of them under their own native appellations, both those which the soil of the earth produce, and those which the trained hand of the skilful workman knew how to fashion for the wants of war or peace. We are astonished at the countless riches which were laid up in the treasuries of the temples. These same inscriptions on the stone walls of the temples, which, then in a better state of preservation, the wise men of Thebes once read and explained to the Emperor Germanicus, on his visit to the Amon city, still to this day confirm to us what Tacitus has related. " There was read "—thus states the Roman historian—" the tributes imposed on the nations, the weight in silver and gold, the number of weapons and horses, and the presents in ivory and sweet scents given to the temples, how much wheat and effects of all sorts, each nation had to provide, in truth not less great than what at present the power of the Parthian or the Roman might imposes." '

It was A. D. 19 that Germanicus visited Egypt, a little while before his lamented death. The treasures of monumental information which the long reign of this Pharaoh has bequeathed to us almost exceed description : and the historical and geographical data which he has left us, extending right round the vast circuit from the Soudan, Somâli land, through Palestine and Northern Syria, across the Euphrates, and down its course to Chaldæa, are even yet imperfectly studied and un-

developed in their full results. Indeed, it has been
rather the fashion to view as boastful exaggeration the
records of these conquests, until the recent acquisition of
the cuneiform despatches of Tel-el-Amarna forced us to
the conclusion that the actual sovereignty of this vast
region, comprising the full circuit of the ancient empires,
lay in the hands of successive Pharaohs of this great
XVIIIth dynasty. It required more than thirteen campaigns to bring about this submission, and to bring in
the steady streams of tribute from Assur, Babel, the
Ruten of Syria, the mountaineers of the Lebanon,
the coast cities of Phœnicia, the island of Cyprus,
the wild wanderers of the Sinaitic peninsula and the
Arabian deserts, the Amorites and the Hittites, the
mingled races of Cush, and of the coast-lands of the
Red Sea.

Amenhotep II., son and successor of Thothmes III.,
made war in the Euphrates-region, and we find him at
Nii in the north, as well as opposite to the Palmyra district of later days. His successor and son Thothmes
IV. made war against the Kheta, from whom Thothmes
III. had received tribute, and had with him a valiant
staff officer, a successor of Aahmes and Amen-em-heb,
named Amenhotep, who fought by his side from Naharina in the north to Galla-land in Africa.

The same far-reaching empire owned the sway of the
next Pharaoh, the celebrated Amenhotep III., whose
vast twin statues cast their shadows across the plain of
Thebes, and whose dealings with the river-land of Naharina were still more important than those of the kings
before him ; for, although his wars were mostly in Kush,
it was in Naharina that he hunted and slew 210 lions,

and won his beloved queen Taïa, daughter of Iuâ and his wife Tuâ. The differences of opinion with regard to the race to which this king's mother belonged are now laid at rest by the Tel-el-Amarna tablets, in which we find that her father was King of Mitâni, which was a part of the region called by the Egyptians Naharina, between the Euphrates and the Belîkh river. Her nephew was named Dûsratta, and in his turn became king; and a daughter of that prince became the wife of her cousin Amenhotep IV., the renowned patron of a rival worship in Egypt, which was intended to supplant the old Egyptian gods with their temples and hierarchies. This was the cultus of the solar disk under the name Aten, from which he assumed the name Khu-en-Aten, glory of Aten ; and, since he could not induce the Thebans to give up their worship of Amen for the new religion, he built a new capital, which after a short life fell into ruins, and is now called Tel-el-Amarna.

There has been a very interesting controversy as to the real origin of this worship, which had been supposed to be an importation from Syria and connected with the worship of Adonis, or, at all events, Aten was taken as equivalent to the Semitic *adon* (אדון, or אדן), 'lord.'

But Professor Maspero has repudiated all such notions, and strongly insisted that Taïa was a high-born Egyptian lady, and no foreigner, and that the Aten-cult was not exotic at all, but home-born and long established in the land. M. Bouriant has taken the same view[1], but admits that 'in strictness this word (*aten*) might be a transcrip-

---

[1] *Rec. de Travaux*, vol. vi. p. 51.

tion of Adonaï or Adonis ; it even ought to be so (*il a dû mème en être ainsi*), if Amenhotep IV. was truly a Semite.'

This is a very interesting admission, for we are now aware that his mother Taïa was indeed a princess of Mesopotamia, and his own wife was her niece [1].   This fact, by the way, accounts for the almost ludicrous uniformity of the faces of the king and queen in those quaint relief-sculptures which have so stimulated the fancy of Egyptologists.

Although, as M. Bouriant pleads, there are proofs at Gizeh of Aten-worship before the reign of this Pharaoh, they only seem to indicate its gradual introduction under Taïa's influence, albeit not only at Thebes but at Heliopolis also, where M. Maspero considers that it was an ancient form of the Râ-cultus, ' the most ancient probably [2].'   Is it not possible that this, with its coincidence or consonance of name, was made the groundwork for a development of Mesopotamian observances ; as the old Egyptian Set became the Hyksôs and Hittite god Sutekh, equally called Set or Sut ?

Tammuz (Dumuzi), called Adonai, was a sun-god whose worship might well be grounded on an old Adon-ritual of On ; and it is worthy of remark that the Syrian scribes writing from Naharina address the Pharaohs Amenhotep III. and IV. as ' my sun-god and the god of heaven' (Samsi-ya u il śame), and speak of ' business with the house of the sun-god' (bit sa Samsi).

In some scenes of worship on Assyrian cylinders, we find long undulating rays like ribbons proceeding from

---

[1] See *Zeitschrift f. Aeg. Spr.* 1890, 112–114.
[2] *Hist.* p. 211, 4th ed.

the winged disk, and ending in a bifurcation. Kings or pontiffs, with right hand uplifted in adoration, take hold with the left hand of these symbolic rays, or whatsoever they may be. Did any such motive lead to the rays of the Aten-disk outstretched with hands, often full of gifts of life and other blessings [1]?

Be these things as they may, it seems now fairly established, that the development of this exclusive cultus at least is due to the Mesopotamian marriages in two generations of Amenhoteps.

Dr. Birch, with his characteristic thoughtful caution, writes thus in a very important and interesting article in the *Archæological Journal*, 1851, p. 405 : 'In the reign of Amenophis (III.), as already mentioned, the worship of the *Aten*, or Aten-ra, the sun's disk or orb, first appears.

This name, which resembles that of the Hebrew אדן, Adonai or Lord, and the Syrian Adonis, appears to have been either a foreign religion introduced into Egypt, or else a part of the sun-worship which had assumed an undue influence or development.'

The celebrated queen's name appears in the cuneiform as Te-i-e. She has been confused in a regrettable way by some writers with a beautiful queen of much later time, the consort of Set-nekht, whose name was Titi.

In one of the Tel-el-Amarna letters, the writer Aziru addresses his 'father' Dûdu as a person of high authority at court, 'a fact,' as Professor Sayce says, 'which shows the high position held in Egypt by Semites belonging to the Canaanite, if not to the Hebrew race, at the close

[1] Perrot et Chipiez, *Art in Chaldæa*, vol. ii. p. 273, cf. p. 261.

of the XVIIIth dynasty. . . . Aziru, the son of Dûdu, is probably the officer mentioned in XII, 8, [another tablet], who was the representative of the Pharaoh in Phœnicia.'

Now at Tel-el-Amarna is a tomb of Tutu, with a fine hymn to Aten; and in the British Museum is 'a sepulchral tablet of Tutu, on which is seen an adoration to the hawk-headed god Horus[1].' I think these belong to the same officer, who may well be the Dûdu of the tablet. This name is, as Prof. Sayce has pointed out, identical with Dûd, Daûd, David, which, indeed, we have in the Old Testament in the form Dudu (Dodo).

Dr. Kellogg in his interesting lectures[2] has assigned to Joseph's government the time of Thothmes III., and ascribes to his influence 'that curious marriage of the third Amenophis, that undoubtedly can be adequately explained by the presence of some of Joseph's kindred in the court circle.' Now, although this chronology is untenable, yet it may be thought that the influence of Joseph may have coalesced with other Semitic tendencies under the hand of Queen Taïa and her niece and daughter-in-law to break up the power of the Theban hierarchy of Amen, and supplant it by a new system of Heliopolitan affinity. And perhaps a great court-officer of so Hebraic a name as Dudu may have come from that quarter. At any rate every such datum tells in favour of the belief that it was not a Pharaoh of the XVIIIth dynasty, 'who knew not Joseph;' but, as Prof. Sayce says: 'The rise of the

---

[1] Wiedemann, *Geschichte*, pp. 401, 406. Birch, *Arch. Journal*, 1851, p. 409.

[2] *Abraham, Joseph, and Moses in Egypt*; New York, 1887.

XIXth dynasty marks the reaction against the Semitic faith and surroundings of Amenophis IV., and explains the statement of Exodus i. 8[1].'

These considerations give a fresh and peculiar interest to the study of those strange tableaux of the Aten-period, and we look at the cringing figures and aquiline countenances of the high ministers in attendance on the un-Egyptian king and queen under a new light. Indeed, they were exotic potentates, for Amenhotep III. had a mother a princess of Naharina, Mût-em-ua, whose features he bore, and not those of his father Thothmes IV. And he, himself half foreign, had a son three-quarters foreign, who married a wife entirely Mesopotamian. Thus the drift had been great and rapid, and once more the old stock of the Egyptian aristocracy and hierarchy found themselves 'among new men, strange faces, other minds.' The 'strange faces' may be seen in the fine engravings of Prisse, or, more easily, in some illustrations given by Mr. Villiers Stuart[2].

As to the king himself, I account for his features as inherited from his grandmother and father, on the one hand, and on the other from the Semitic line of Taïa, his mother ; and his ungainly figure is misshapen by the obesity so well known in Ethiopia, and so grotesquely shown in the figure of the queen of Pûn and her daughter in the reliefs of Deir-el-Bahri[3].

Brugsch has given a very lively and pleasant picture

---

[1] *Proc. S. Bib. Arch.* 1889, p. 344.

[2] *Nile Gleanings*, p. 300 ; *Funeral Tent of an Egyptian Queen*, p. 99.

[3] Cf. my paper on ethnographic types of Mr. Flinders Petrie's collection (*Anthropol. Journal*, 1888, p. 220).

of the affectionate family-life of this royal household, and of their devotions, in which they adored in the radiant orb of the sun the creator and nourisher of all things. Some of the ascriptions, were they only addressed to God Himself, remind us vividly of the psalms that celebrate the divine handiwork in Nature. Here is an example from the tomb of Aahmes, master of the royal household in the new capital: 'Beautiful is thy setting, thou Sun's disk [Aten] of life, thou lord of lords, and king of the worlds. When thou unitest thyself with the heaven at thy setting, mortals rejoice before thy countenance, and give honour to him who has created them, and pray before him who has formed them, before the glance of thy son, who loves thee, the king Khunaten. The whole land of Egypt and all peoples repeat all thy names at thy rising, to magnify thy rising in like manner as thy setting. Thou, O god, who in truth art the living one, standest before the two eyes. Thou art he which createst what never was, which formest everything, which art in all things; we also have come into being through the word of thy mouth[1].'

The learned Egyptologist thus comments: 'In these and similar creations of a poetic form there reigns such a depth of view, and so devout a conception of God, that we are almost inclined to give our complete assent to the teaching about which the king is wont to speak so fully and with so much pleasure.'

---

[1] The best view of the matter, perhaps, is suggested by such phrases as this in a hymn of the time of Har-em-heb, of whom we shall speak presently: 'the king of gods . . . he is Râ, his body the sun's orb (*aten*), he is in eternity' (Meyer, *Geschichte des alten Aegyptens*, 1887, p. 274).

But Job says: 'If I beheld the sun when it shined, or the moon walking in brightness; and my heart hath been secretly enticed, or my mouth hath kissed my hand: this also were an iniquity to be punished by the judge: for I should have denied the God that is above[1].'

It is very curious to contrast with Brugsch's impression the verdict of our own lamented Birch, who says of Amenhotep III. : 'His son, Amenhotep IV., who had been appointed in the lifetime of his father, became an heretical fanatic of the worst sort. He carried the worship of the " disk," or Aten, to its extreme limits, and persecuted all other forms of deities except those of the purely solar gods[2].'

It is worth while to notice that if the queen Mût-em-ua, wife of Thothmes IV., and mother of Amenhotep III., were connected with Pûn, as seems so likely, then her descendants would be likely from her to learn affiance to solar worship, so characteristic of the people of that land. 'The ancient religion of Yemen,' says Lenormant, 'was specially solar. In the sun the Sabæans saw the highest, purest, and most complete manifestation of the divine being, and they adored it as the special manifestation of divinity[3].'

Not long after the death of Khu-en-Aten, a great reaction in favour of the old system of Amen-worship of Thebes brought about the collapse of the rival cultus and hierarchy. After several obscure potentates ennobled by royal marriages we come to a distinguished

---

[1] Job xxxi. 26–28.   [2] *Hist. of Egypt, p.* 109.
[3] *Anc. Hist. of the East*, vol. ii. p. 323.

ruler who had been a chief officer of the highest rank, Har-em-heb by name. He returned to the old allegiance in religion, and destroyed the short-lived splendour of the rival capital. Then came, in some way not well explained, the transition from the XVIIIth to the XIXth dynasty, which is signalized by the Pharaonic names Râmeses and Seti.

CHAPTER XIV.

RÂMESES I. and his son Seti I. reigned together, but before long Seti succeeded on his father's death. And then begins in earnest the new *régime*.

The usual result of changes in the government had taken place on the eastern frontier, and risings of subject nations in Syria called the king to arms.

Meanwhile the Hebrews had thriven and multiplied since ' Joseph, and all his brethren, and all that generation' had been gathered to their fathers; 'and the land was filled with them;' that is, as Canon Cook says, ' the district allotted to them, extending probably from the eastern branch of the Nile to the borders of the desert. It appears from other passages (see Ex. iii. 22) that they did not occupy this ground exclusively, but were intermingled with the native Egyptians.' They were also intermingled with men of many races, as we may now say with increasing certainty, with Phœnicians of the coast, with the groundlings of the Hyksôs hordes who were left when their lords and military levies were driven out ; with Libyans of the West, and nomads of the East,

the Shasu of the Egyptian inscriptions, with adventurers
of the Mediterranean coasts and islands : but it appears
that the Hebrews, whose grant of Goshen was as yet
unrepealed, were the most powerful element in this
cosmopolitan state of affairs.

In some valuable papers of Mr. Reginald Stuart
Poole, published in the *Contemporary Review* in 1879,
he thus writes : 'Unfortunately we do not know the
duration of the oppression of the Israelites, nor the condition of Lower Egypt during the XVIIIth dynasty,
which, according to the hypothesis here adopted, corresponds to a great part of the Hebrew sojourn.   It is,
however, clear from the Bible that the oppression did
not begin till after the period of Joseph's contemporaries,
and had lasted eighty years before the Exodus.   It
seems almost certain that this was the actual beginning
of the oppression, for it is very improbable that two
separate Pharaohs are intended by "the new king which
knew not Joseph" and the builder of Râmeses, or, in
other words, Râmeses II.   And the time from the accession of Râmeses II. to the end of Menptah's reign can have
little exceeded the eighty years of Scripture between the
birth of Moses and the Exodus.

'The Egyptian monuments are almost silent as to
Lower Egypt from the time of Aahmes, conqueror of the
Shepherds, to that of Râmeses II. Whether the kings of
the XVIIIth dynasty oppressed or tolerated the Shemite
population we do not know.   Under the XIXth dynasty,
not impossibly of partly Shepherd race, Tanis is re-
founded, and the whole of the east of Lower Egypt is
adorned with temples, and specially strengthened with
forts.   Semitic ideas come into fashion.   The new

literary activity may well be due to contact with Shemites. This might seem strange of a time of persecution,
but we must reflect that it implies a long previous contact of two nationalities, and that precisely what we
observe in the Semitic character of the Egyptian of the
XIXth dynasty is conversely true of the Hebrew of the
same age, which is coloured by Egyptian, though far less
markedly. The contact had its effect on both sides.'

It is a very important and curious parallel between the
silence of Egyptian monuments as to Lower Egypt from
the expulsion of the Hyksôs to the reign of Râmeses II.,
and the corresponding chasm in the Scripture history,
which is only partially bridged by the information of the
increase and prosperity of the Israelites until the rise of
the new king. There is a curious gleam of light in
1 Chron. vii. 21, 22, where some sons of Ephraim are
mentioned, 'whom the men of Gath born in the land
slew, because they came down to take away their cattle.
And Ephraim their father mourned many days, and his
brethren came to comfort him.' This episode is very
interesting indeed, for it shows that during the lifetime
of Joseph's younger son, the Israelites were able to make
a warlike expedition as far as Gath, without any hin-
drance from the Egyptian authorities in crossing the
frontier on their way out or their return. This agrees
with the account of their power and prosperity.

It is to be remembered that Ephraim and his brother
were not only sons of Joseph, but of a very noble Egyptian lady, and they would be powerful and eminent
accordingly.

By 'the men of Gath born in the land' the writer of
the Book of Chronicles probably meant to discriminate

between the Canaanite inhabitants of old date and the later Philistine masters of this part of Palestine. Then there follows a singular statement of the birth of Beriah, a subsequent son of Ephraim, 'and his daughter was Sherah, who built Beth-horon the nether, and the upper, and Uzzen-Sherah.' These were ancestors of Joshua. On this passage Professor Rawlinson comments: 'It is not clear whether Sherah is to be regarded as a daughter of Beriah or a daughter of Ephraim. In either case, she could scarcely herself have built the Palestinian cities here mentioned, which must belong to a time not earlier than Joshua. By " she built " we must understand " her descendants built." ' But I would rather take the statement as it stands, and believe that Ephraim's daughter, or granddaughter, had possessions in the hill-country, and built these places.

Dr. Mahler, on astronomical grounds, makes the reign of Thothmes III. begin in B.C. 1503 and end in 1449. These are landmarks. Both before and after his time Egypt was in full lordship of Palestine and Syria, and it would be hard to say that a granddaughter or great-granddaughter of Asenath could not have occupied ground in that condition of things and made settlements in the land of Canaan. This also re-opens the inquiry as to Jacob-el and Joseph-el, and the occupation of those localities, or the significance of those names in the list of Thothmes.

We must take account of the latest results of M. Naville's work in qualifying our opinion as to the presence of the XVIIIth dynasty in the Delta. He writes :—'In spite of the successes of the kings of the XVIIth dynasty, Sekenen-Râ and Amosis, the expulsion of the Hyksôs and the restoration of the Egyptian rule over the Delta took place only gradually. A queen of the XVIIIth dynasty alludes in one of her inscriptions to the harm done in the country by the strangers, and which she endeavoured to repair. A proof of the fact that the Egyptian dominion was not yet regularly re-established was the total absence of monuments of the XVIIIth dynasty in the Delta. Until now there was only one known,—a stone serpent found at Benha, or a few scarabs of Amenophis III., dug out by the fellahîn at Tel Basta. The desire to settle, if possible, this question of the presence of the XVIIIth dynasty in the Delta, was one of the chief reasons which induced me to dig at Bubastis ; and in this respect my expectation has not been frustrated ; we have discovered important monuments of the XVIIIth dynasty at Tel Basta ; last summer, also, the fellahîn came across a large tablet of the same dynasty at Samanood, further north. In both places the monuments are later than Thothmes III. It seems very probable that the final conquest of the Delta and the complete expulsion of the Hyksôs dates from the great wars of Thothmes III., justly called "the Great," or sometimes the Alexander of Egypt. His campaign had lasting results, not only in Egypt, but also abroad, as we know now from the curious find of cuneiform tablets made by the Arabs of Tel-el-Amarna last year,—that under the successors of Thothmes III., a great many Syrian cities were still tributary to Egypt, and had Egyptian governors. The most ancient mention of a king of the XVIIIth dynasty is on a stone of Amenophis II., who is sculptured standing before Amon Ra and making him offerings. We notice here, as under the following kings, that the chief divinity of the place is not Bast, but Amon. The king of the XVIIIth dynasty who seems to have taken the greatest interest in Bubastis is Amenophis III. We discovered four monuments of the reign of this king; two of them are statues of the same man. . . . . " prince of the first order, a friend loving his lord, chief of the works of his king in the provinces of the marsh land of the north, the chancellor and city governor, Amenophis." The name of his king is found on the back; the braces which support his garments are tied together by a brooch on which is engraved the name of Amenophis III.; another statue has it engraved on the shoulder, as well as a very graceful torso of a woman, which was part of a double group of a priest and priestess. Thus the XVIIIth dynasty is well represented at Bubastis,—its high officers and priests put their images in the temple. Even the heretical king Amenophis IV., or Khuenaten, who endeavoured to destroy the worship of Amon, desired his name to be at Bubastis. On a stone, usurped afterwards by Râmeses II., we read the name of his god, his own cartouche having been erased. In what state did the XVIIIth dynasty find the temple of Bubastis? Had it been ruined by the Hyksôs? Not likely; on the contrary, we have seen that Apepi raised there his statue, and besides, as he says, pillars in great numbers and bronze doors. If it did not suffer in the wars between the Hyksôs and the Theban princes, the temple must have been standing and even of a remarkable beauty when the contemporaries of Amenophis III. put their statues in its halls[1].'

[1] *The Historical Results of the Excavations of Bubastis.* Trans. of Victoria Institute, July 5, 1889, p. 18.

The views expressed by Lenormant appear to be just and sagacious: 'The stranger kings had been driven out of Lower Egypt; the unity of the country and its full independence had been re-established ; a native dynasty, a glorious dynasty, warlike and victorious, had mounted the throne. These kings appear to have left the Hebrews in peace, and even to have favoured them. It even seems that the children of Israel were concerned on several occasions in the early Asiatic campaigns of that dynasty, and had taken advantage of that circumstance to attempt to make settlements in the land promised to their race—attempts which failed. Thus mention is made of an expedition of the sons of Ephraim against the people of Gath, whose cattle they tried to drive off, but who slew them (1 Chron. vii. 21). A daughter of Ephraim built several cities in the land of Canaan, (1 Chron. vii. 24). Lastly it is mentioned that the family of Shelah, son of Judah, had made conquests on the territory of Moab (1 Chron. iv. 21, 22)[1].'

But with the XIXth dynasty came the evil days and more especially with the long reign of sixty-seven years of Râmeses II., whose ambitious and luxurious magnificence made him towards his own people and all

---

[1] *Ancient History of the East*, vol. i. p. 91. It may be well to notice that the foreign brickmakers depicted in the well-known wall-paintings of the tomb of Rekhmara at Thebes are Syrian captives of Thothmes III., not Jews ; as Sir Gardner Wilkinson has pointed out (*Ancient Egyptians*, 1869, vol. i. p. 345. Dr. Wiedemann writes on this point : ' Though this representation has nothing to do with the Bible and the Jews, however it may have been so pretended (*p. ex.* by Hengstenberg, *Die Bücher Mose's und Aegypten*, p. 79 sq., and Kurtz, *Gesch. des alten Bundes*, vol. ii. p. 25 sq.), it gives a complete illustration of the subject, and corresponds in all its details with the Biblical records (*Pr. S. Bib. Arch.* 1888, p. 36).

others within his reach and grasp most emphatically the oppressive Pharaoh.

The invaluable results of M. Naville's excavations at Tel-el-Maskhûta have made manifest the rectitude of the late M. Chabas's conclusions in his fine Memoir on the XIXth dynasty and the Exodus; and the handiwork of the enslaved Hebrews is to be seen and handled at Pithom. It is to be hoped that the works of the Egypt Exploration Fund Committee will be worthily appreciated and supported in Great Britain, as they are by our brethren on the other side of the blue water, who are at present even contributing the larger share of the cost, and certainly showing that animated interest in the work which is characteristic of American scholars. It was even, I believe, through an excess of incredulity that the 'statue of flesh' which still remains as the bodily memorial of Râmeses, escaped a long migration across the ocean and a resting-place in America.

Two great and prominent features of the era of the XIXth dynasty are to be remembered. The one is that the centre of gravity of the empire was once more established in the Delta, and especially in the 'field of Zoan;' the other that in Syria the mastery of that remarkable people the Kheta (Hittites) had overpowered the old Aramaic domination, and that now it was even a question of serious uncertainty whether Egypt could hold its own, or whether a new system of Asiatic aliens should bring back the days of the Hyksôs Pharaohs and the worship of Sutekh. The worship, indeed, in a very strange and significant way did return in great strength, perhaps as a politic concession to the habits and likings of the eastern population of Lower Egypt. But the

Hittites and their close allies the Amorites were now (as in the Scriptural account) the power with whom Egypt had to reckon as its rival, and with whom by treaty and marriage (as in the former doings with Naharina) a bond was formed, which has great significance for us as students of this scroll of ancient history.

We must not, however, be tempted to transgress our proper limit, and enter on the life and work of Moses.

To exhibit the more clearly the last result of evidence so lately acquired, we will once more turn to an able summary by Professor Sayce, in which he puts the matter well before the eyes of the general student[1]:—

'The Egyptian garrisons in Syria and Palestine had been withdrawn, and the cities of Canaan were once more independent. There was no longer the strong arm of Egypt to protect them from their northern foes. Syria was overrun by the Hittite tribes, and the sacred city of Kadesh on the Orontes, between Damascus and Hamath, became a Hittite stronghold. The Semites of the east were cut off from their brethren of the west, and the literary and commercial intercourse between Palestine and the countries beyond the Euphrates was destroyed. The first three monarchs of the XIXth dynasty—Ramses I., Seti I., and Ramses II.—vainly endeavoured to expel the Hittite invader. Though Ramses II. forced the Canaanitish cities again to acknowledge the suzerainty of Egypt, twenty long years of warfare brought him no decisive victory over his Hittite foes. He was fain to conclude peace with them on equal terms, and the treaty between himself and the " great King of

[1] 'Letters from Palestine before the Age of Moses,' *Newbury House Magazine*, 1889, p. 261.

the Hittites" is one of the most curious monuments that ancient history has bequeathed to us.

'The wars of Ramses, however, brought desolation to Canaan. The Canaanitish princes stood between two opposing forces, and suffered accordingly. When the Israelites arrived, after the death of the great Egyptian monarch, they found an exhausted population, little able to withstand their attack. The Hittite wars of Ramses, in fact, prepared the way for the Israelitish conquest of Canaan. Rameses II. was the Pharaoh of the oppression. Egyptian scholars long ago maintained that the Exodus could not have taken place till after his death, and M. Naville's discovery of Pithom has proved that they were right. Pithom was one of the "treasure cities" built by the Israelites in Egypt (Exodus i. 11), and the monuments of the city inform us that its founder was Ramses. The tablets of Tel-el-Amarna have now come to confirm the conclusion, and to explain why it is that Scripture takes no notice of the long period of time occupied by the rule of the XVIIIth dynasty. We gather from them that it was not until the overthrow of the XVIIIth dynasty that the Semitic stranger ceased to be honoured and powerful in the land of Egypt. The court itself was more than half Semitic, and the governors and officials of the Egyptian king were for the most part of Semitic descent. . . .

'The rise of the XIXth dynasty marks the reaction against the policy and principles of Khu-n-Aten, and the successful revolt of the Egyptian people. The Semite was expelled or crushed as completely as the European would have been in recent years, had the revolt of Arabi succeeded. It is, accordingly, in the

founder of the XIXth dynasty that we must look for
the new king "which knew not Joseph" (Exodus i. 8).
The oppression did not last for centuries; at most it
could have covered a period of only a hundred years,
the greater, part of which was occupied by the sixty-
seven years' reign of Ramses II. The two cities which
he built were the two which we are told were erected
by Israelitish labour; the sacred historian, at least,
knows of no others. At last, therefore, we have found
solid standing-ground in Egyptian history for the
events which issued in the Exodus.'

It is a very interesting inquiry, What was the origin
of the queen of Seti I., and mother of Râmeses II., whom
Seti had married before he came to the throne, and who
survived Seti[1]? Her name was Tuia, identical with
that of the mother of Queen Taïa (Teie); and it has
been thought by Brugsch and Maspero that Seti's
queen was of that genealogy. Râmeses I., father of
Seti, had been in the service of Aï and Har-em-heb,
and Maspero conjectures that the princess was a
daughter of Amenhotep III.[2]

Meyer thinks that Râmeses I. was very likely Har-
em-heb's brother. The very handsome features of the
Ramesside kings of the XIXth dynasty strike us as not
purely Egyptian, but of Semitic affinity, and, as it now
seems, Aramaic. The name Tuia appears almost identical with that of Toï or Toü (תעי, תעו), King of Hamath,
the ally of David[3].

According to the calculations adduced by Brugsch,

---

[1] Maspero, *Pr. S. B. Arch.* 1889, p. 194.   [2] *Hist.* p. 217.

[3] 'Tuya,' writes Prof. Sayce to me, 'is the name of an Amorite in the
Tel-el-Amarna tablets.'

the end of the reign of Râmeses II. and accession of
Mer-en-ptah took place in the year B.C. 1280, and
it seems most probable that the Exodus happened in
his reign. And we are told that 'Moses took the
bones of Joseph with him, for he had straitly sworn
the children of Israel, saying, God will surely visit you ;
and ye shall carry up my bones away hence with you[1].'

It is a very curious thing that Chærêmôn, as quoted
by Josephus in his controversy against Apion (I. 32), says
that Joseph, whose Egyptian name had been Petesêph
(Πετεσήφ), with Moses, who had been a scribe like
Joseph (who, however, was a sacred scribe), together
led the Hebrews in their Exodus. Osarsiph, says
Manetho, was born at Heliopolis, and was called so
from Osiris, who was the god of Heliopolis; but when
he was gone over to these people his name was changed,
and he was called Moses. As to these names, reported
by the Egyptian priestly historian of Sebennytus, in the
time of Ptolemy I. (Sôtêr), from B.C. 323 to 283, and
the historian Chærêmôn, of the time of Nero, they
are truly Egyptian in character, and (as I pointed out
in 1880) have the last element in common with the
name Joseph, as far as an Egyptian would know who
was unacquainted with Semitic names. As to Moses,
who was so called by the princess who saved him,
when 'he became her son,' it is generally supposed
by Egyptologists that the name Mosheh (משה) represents the Egyptian word Mesu, ' son,' which was used
as a proper name. But he may have borne the name
Osarsiph (Οσαρσιφ) as well, and it is quite true that
Osiris bore the title Osar-sapi. The name applied to

___
[1] Ex. xiii. 19.

Joseph, Peteseph, would mean the gift of a certain god, either (as I suggested) the god of the Arabian nome, Sapt, whose name remains at the site of the old capital Pi-saptu, now called Saft, as we have seen in our account of Goshen ; or (as Professor Maspero proposed to me) the god Sapi, equivalent to the title of Osar-sapi. In fact, the latter explanation has been put forward by Dr. Ebers [1].

The name of the town of Sapi is mentioned in connection with Osiris ('the town of Sep') on the Turin altar of Pepi of the VIth dynasty.

But the apparently wild statement that both Joseph and Moses led the Exodus of the children of Israel seems to be very well explained by the fact that the dead ruler of the golden ages accompanied the living leader through all the weary marches to the Land of Promise. And, so understood, the statement of Chærêmôn coincides with the narrative of Holy Scripture.

It was 'by faith,' and with the highest motives, that Joseph had given commandment concerning his bones; but the actual fulfilment of his behest not unnaturally reminds us of the strange episode in our own Scottish wars, when the old warlike English King Edward I., no longer living, led the army of his people, according to his dying injunction ;—a parallel which has an interest in the great contrast of character between the two heroes of national history.

The unexpected and most abundant elucidation of the whole history of Joseph, from his entrance as a slave to his sublime exit in the midst of his descendants, which Egypt has afforded in these so distant days, may be

[1] *Durch Gosen zum Sinaï*, 2nd ed., p. 561.

very profitably compared with the slender aid rendered in the matter by Assyriology.   In Schrader's exhaustive commentary, drawn from that source, there is scarcely anything that bears upon the life of Joseph or the Exodus.

In further illustration of our extended view, a few points in which light may be thrown on the history from Egyptian sources may now be mentioned.   Perhaps the cruel device for destroying the Hebrew race by infanticide may be no great subject for surprise in an Eastern despot.   But I am not sure that there may not be under our eyes an ancient instance of the kind.   For among the discoveries of Mr. Flinders Petrie at Kahun, in the Fayûm, a town constructed for workmen in the time of Usertasen II., of the XIIth dynasty, where a great number of foreign people were stationed and employed, there were found buried in some of the houses boxes containing the bodies of infants, who, it is stated, had been put to death.   But the poor parents had buried them with affectionate solicitude, putting beside them ornaments and toys, according to the Egyptian usage.   It has occurred to my mind that possibly some destruction of the innocents by despotic order may have taken place among the captive strangers in this early settlement.

In the other scene of Mr. Petrie's last excavation in the Fayûm, Tel Gurob, most interesting relics of foreigners were found.   This town brings us down to the time of the Hebrew oppression and Exodus, and, like the former settlement of a time long before Abraham, again contains abundant evidences of the sojourn of foreigners, both Hittites and strangers from the Mediterranean coast-peoples ; and it was broken up at the time when Merenptah, after the great unsuccessful invasion of the Libyan confederation, expelled the foreigners from his dominions. Gurob then is of the same date as Pithom, and appears to bear similar testimony.

M. Naville is not only of opinion that the Exodus took place in the reign of Merenptah (who, by the way, is known from Egyptian sources to have been greatly under the sway of the magicians, like his elder brother Kha-em-uas); but he writes: 'The kingdom was much weakened by the long wars which Râmeses II. had waged without much result against his Asiatic neighbours, and also by his tyrannical and wasteful rule; so much so that in the fifth year of Merenptah a coalition of nations of the Mediterranean invaded Egypt, and very nearly reached Memphis. It is during the troubles and the difficulties which beset Merenptah in the beginning of his reign that the Exodus must have taken place.'

It is among the points of great interest involved in the fresh examination of the ruins of Bubastis, that, as it is now found to have been one of the chief seats of the court of Apepi in the time of Joseph, so also it must have been a principal centre of the power of Râmeses II., with whom, as M. Naville writes, 'we reach a period of great [monumental] changes, which consisted chiefly in usurpations. There is no name which occurs so frequently in the ruins of the first three halls, which up to the XIIIth dynasty constituted the whole building. As is the case in Tanis, the local divinity seems to have occupied only a secondary rank; all the principal offerings or acts of worship take place before the great gods of Egypt, Amon, Phtah, called Phtah of Râmeses, and chiefly Set, the god of the Hyksôs, who had the most

prominent place.   Enormous architraves in the second
hall bear dedications to Set ; elsewhere he is styled Set
of Râmeses, and his face was engraved on all the palm
capital columns, where it was afterwards transformed to
Mahes.   Nevertheless Bast appears sometimes in the
inscriptions of Râmeses II.,—for instance, on a great
tablet, of which we found only a part, and which is a
dialogue between the king and a goddess, who makes
his eulogy in words like the following : " I take in my
hand the timbrel, and I celebrate thy coming forth, for
thou hast multiplied the sacred things millions of times."

'There is no question that Râmeses II. worked much
in Bubastis ; but in the way which best illustrates his
personal character, and the tendency of all his acts.
An extraordinary vanity and self-conceit, a violent desire
to dazzle his contemporaries by his display, and posterity
by the immense number of constructions there in his
name, seems to have been the ruling power of his conduct
during his long reign.   In the second hall of Bubastis
there are many colossal architraves where his cartouche
is engraved in letters several feet high ; there is not one
of them where an older inscription has not been cut out,
sometimes the old signs are still visible,—once also, very
likely because something concealed the end of the stone,
the workman did not take the trouble to erase completely,
and at the end of the cartouche of Râmeses II., appear
the first letters of the name Usertesen III., of the XIIth
dynasty.

'There is no doubt that Bubastis was a place for which
Râmeses felt a special liking ; he was anxious that the
whole temple should appear as built by himself, from the
great statues of Apepi at the entrance to the columns of

the hypostyle hall at the western side. I do not believe
that there are other temples with so many statues bearing
the name of Râmeses II. as Bubastis. Undoubtedly
they have not all been made for him ; two of the finest
which we discovered, both in black granite, were certainly
not his portrait. . . . They are kings of the XIIIth or
XIVth dynasty. . . . The more we study the remains
of Bubastis, the more we are convinced that the place
must have been one of the favourite resorts of Râmeses
II., where he stayed repeatedly. Bubastis and Tanis were
the two great cities of the Delta, and no doubt the court
came frequently to both places. Râmeses was accompanied by his sons ; one of them, Kha-em-uas, who had
a high rank in the priesthood, and who was inspector of
temples, has recorded his visit to Bubastis on a statue of
his father.

'We found also the mention of two others, who had
military commands. One, whose statue is in Boston,
was "first cavalry officer of his father, the chief of the
horse of his majesty, Menthouhershopshef ; " the other,
who became the king of the Exodus, was at that time
a general of infantry ; and he appears several times on
sculptures making offerings to the god Amon. . . . It has
been the result of my first campaign of excavations, to
discover the site of Pithom, not very far from the present
city of Ismaïlah ; Râmeses is not yet known ; it is very
likely between Pithom and Bubastis, in the Wadi
Tumilat.

'I cannot dwell at great length here on the events of
the Exodus ; yet I should like to mention that the
successive discoveries made in the Delta have had the
result of making the sacred narrative more compre-

hensible in many points, and in one especially—in showing that the distances were much shorter than was generally thought. I consider, for instance, it important to have established that Bubastis was a very large city, and a favourite resort of the king and his family. It is quite possible that at the time when the events preceding the Exodus took place, the king was at Bubastis, not at Tanis, as we generally believed.

'Menephthah, the king of the Exodus, who is represented as general of infantry, executed also statues in the temple after he became king, but they are very much broken.'

In making the foregoing copious quotation from our excellent and learned discoverer, I am persuaded that there is no need of excuse. We now possess the detailed report of M. Naville's work, and much of very high interest is clearly established. To appreciate this a little, it only needs to turn to the valuable little book of Dr. Reginald Stuart Poole, *The Cities of Egypt*. He tells us the interesting fact that Pi-beseth is as old as the second Egyptian dynasty, and refers especially, and almost exclusively, to the Bubastite dynasty, of which the Biblical Shishak was the head. He also anticipates, as all did who are concerned in these excavations, monumental evidence as to the origin and history of that XXIst dynasty. But who imagined the impending discovery of the monuments of the Hyksôs of Joseph's time,—of the great lords of the palmy days of his family,—of the ambitious and self-exalting oppressor, and his son and successor, in whose hands the whole fabric of his despotism so nearly collapsed altogether, and the enslaved Israelites were delivered?

One great point to be remembered is the return of royal power and splendour to the great cities of the Hyksôs, Zoan, where the unrivalled colossus of Râmeses rose high above the whole ranges of colonnades and portals in its shining grandeur, and Pi-beseth, at the inner limit and entrance of the old land of Goshen, which, now channelled and irrigated, organized and patronized, and royally favoured, became the land of Râmeses.

Another circumstance which strikes me as remarkable is this : that of all the Pharaohs, Râmeses II., with his enormous self-inflated personal ambition and vanity, was the man to 'rise up over Egypt,' and, with all the spirit of a ' *new* king,' to ignore, not Joseph only, whose works and character would be well enough known to Aahmes and his great successors, but also to arrogate and usurp all the glory of the illustrious monarchs of the old time before him, suppressing and falsifying their records, and appropriating their works without misgiving or compunction.

And another instructive thought is this. In view of the great part which Pi-beseth played as the Egyptian sacred city nearest to the Israelites of Goshen, and of its special local cultus of Bast, whose degrading worship is so notorious to readers of Herodotus, we may well perceive the full necessity of the Divine canons. As Mr. Poole says : ' The golden calf and the wild dancing multitude rise before our eyes, and we feel with full force the need of those stern prohibitions in which the Law and the Prophets abound [1].

In the midst, and at the deepest midnight, of that great tribulation of despotism, and in the sore corruptions

[1] *Cities of Egypt*, p. 163.

and seductions of Egyptian idolatry, the hour struck, and the words of Joseph fell due for fulfilment: 'God will surely visit you, and bring you out of this land unto the land which He sware to Abraham, to Isaac, and to Jacob; God will surely visit you, and ye shall carry up my bones from hence.'

There is a strange tradition that Joseph was buried at Pi-Sebek (Crocodilopolis) in the Fayûm, and his body taken thence by the Jews at their departure[1]. The people of Israel faithfully carried their great hero and fatherly friend through all their wanderings till in due season they arrived at Shekem. And under the vast echo of the blessings and curses from the hollow sides of Gerizim and of Ebal, lay the bones of Joseph in their Egyptian spicery, brought to be buried in the very field of his father's possession, where the brave boy had been seeking his brethren when he was sent on to his doom at Dothan. And there, in a hidden sepulchre, perhaps Joseph still awaits in the flesh his further destiny.

The present appearance of the Kabr Yûsef (tomb of Joseph) is described by Professor Donaldson, in a short paper in the *Transactions* of the Society of Biblical Archæology[2]:

' There is hardly any spot in Palestine,' he says, ' which combines as this does the tradition of past times and the concurrent assent as to its authenticity of the varied sects, whether Samaritan, Jewish, Turkish, or Christian ; and this is the more remarkable in a country where the struggles of religious strife are so prevalent, and every supposed holy spot is so much the object of violent contention, whether to Greek or Latin. But the truth is,

[1] Murray's *Egypt*, 1880, p. 378.   [2] Vol. ii. p. 80.

that the Christian does not associate with this tomb any special saint-like sanctity, and no superstitious cere- monial or pilgrimage attaches to it.'

Then follows a precise description, with an illustration, of the very modern erections within the little inclosure wall, which was itself rebuilt in 1868 by Mr. Consul Rogers, as an inscription in English testifies. This last fact is told us in the *Memoirs* of the Palestine Survey [1], where it is fur- ther said : ' The tomb itself is rudely shaped, with a ridge along its length at the top, and has a bearing 227°. It is 3 feet high, 6 feet long, and 4 feet broad. There is a sort of pillar, also covered with plaster, at the head, and another at the foot of the tomb, with a cup-shaped hollow in the top of each, where oil-lamps are lighted and incense burnt by the Jews and the Samaritans. The pillars are 21 inches in diameter. That on the south 2 feet 7 inches high; that on the north 3 feet 9 inches. The courtyard measures 18 feet 7 inches square inside. The walls are 1 foot 9 inches thick. On the south is a Mihrab [Mahometan prayer-niche], 2 feet in diameter and 6 feet 3 inches high.

' Above it are two Hebrew inscriptions, both apparently modern [Professor Donaldson says, one Hebrew and the other Samaritan]; a passage in the floor of the enclosure, 4 feet wide, has a level 6 inches lower than the side Diwans or raised platforms. The entrance to the courtyard is from the north, through the ruin of a little square build- ing, with a dome measuring about 22 feet either way, or equal to the new courtyard.'

Professor Donaldson observes : 'When we consider the pious reverence with which Moses and the descend- ants of Joseph conveyed their precious relic from the

[1] Vol. ii. p. 194.

land of bondage, we may conceive that, although the
present erection may be on the spot of its ultimate deposit, it is but reasonable to suppose they followed the
custom of the Egyptians, among whom they had dwelt
so long, and with whose manner of interment they would
have been so well acquainted.   If so, they must have
made a considerable excavation in the ground, consistent
with the exalted position of their forefather.   In this
they must have formed a sepulchral chamber, lining it
with stone, and must therein have laid the embalmed
body, with its wooden sarcophagus or coffin, with becoming funereal rites.   Without making an excavation
it is impossible to ascertain whether any such chamber
still exists, or to discover any further particulars of this
sacred and interesting spot.'

Dr. Geikie mentions that the little enclosure of the
tomb stands 'at the end of a fine row of olive and fig-
trees.'   And in the *Memoirs* of the Palestine Exploration
Fund it is said :—'There is a vine on the north-east
angle of the court-yard.'   The vine is beautifully symbolic.   'Joseph is a fruitful bough. . . . His branches
run over the wall.'

Josephus says with regard to the brethren of Joseph
that at length they died, after they had lived happily in
Egypt.   'Now the posterity and sons of these men,
after some time, carried their bodies, and buried them at
Hebron ; but as to the bones of Joseph, they carried
them into the land of Canaan afterward, when the
Hebrews went out of Egypt, for so had Joseph made
them promise him upon oath [1].'

---

[1] *Antiquities,* II. 8.

I do not know that we can contradict this. If it be true, Joseph must have had special reason for enjoining his descendants to take his bones with them on their day of visitation of God, and departure, and not before.

'By faith Joseph, when his end was nigh, made mention of the departure of the children of Israel ; and gave commandment concerning his bones.' He looked forward, we may think, to those evil days of the new Pharaoh who should arise up over the land of Egypt, and know not Joseph ; and wisely regarded the influence upon his own people of the sacred charge of his embalmed body; which would in itself be a more moving memorial than any testamentary document or muniment of history.

In the *History of Jerusalem and Hebron* [1], by Mûjîr-ed-dîn, we find this account : ' Joseph died in Egypt, and remained buried there till the times of Moses and Pharaoh. But when Moses left this country, leading the children of Israel in the desert, he exhumed the body of Joseph, and carried it with him in the desert till he himself died. Joshua, being come into Syria with the Israelites, buried it near Nablûs, or rather at Hebron, according to a version widely spread among the people ; it is, in fact, at Hebron that his tomb is seen, and is well known. This belief has general currency among the people, and has never been contested. . . . His tomb is found on the holy ground situated behind the enclosure of Solomon, opposite the tomb of Jacob, and near his two forefathers Abraham and Isaac.' It is thought that this attribution of Joseph's burial was originated by

---

[1] Trans. by Henri Sauvaire. Paris, 1876, p. 21.

jealousy of the Samaritans, who possessed the real sepulchre of Joseph.

The surname of 'The Truthteller' is given from old-time to 'our lord Joseph.' It is the same noble memorial by which our King Alfred was known by his people. I do not know whether the Arabic word is capable, like our own 'soothsayer,' of application to the 'diviner.' But at all events the name Joseph has been brought into relation with this title by Professor Sayce, who has been so good as to give me a note on this point of Assyriological research :—

'The Babylonian and Assyrian *asipu* was the "diviner" or "prophet" who accompanied the army, and promised victory, or threatened defeat, to the soldiers. One text speaks of his "delivering prophecies in a secret place." The word was borrowed by later Hebrew under the form of אַשָּׁף (Dan. i. 20, ii. 10, &c.), but in older Hebrew and Canaanite the representative of the Babylonian sibilant would have been *samech*, and not *shin*.

'We learn from the Tel-el-Amarna tablets that the word had travelled to Canaan before the age of Moses. In despatches written from Phœnicia to the Egyptian king mention is made of *isip*, "the prophet," as well as of his *issipputi* or "prophecy." Here the initial *a* has become *i*, so that the Hebrew or Canaanite transliteration of the word would be יסף (or *plene* יוסף). In my Hibbert Lectures I suggested that *asipu* was the original of the Biblical Joseph ; it was objected that the initial letter was different, and that the word could not have been known to the Canaanites. The Tel-el-Amarna tablets have removed both objections.

'If *Joseph* is the Assyro-Babylonian *asipu*, it will

explain why the writer of Genesis did not know the etymology of the name, and accordingly suggested two alternative ones (Gen. xxx. 23, 24).   The *Canaanite* expression "House of Joseph" will also be explained : this would be the Assyrian *bit assaputi* (or *bit isiputi*), "the house of the oracle." '

It is clear enough that, whether the name was given to Joseph with any such reference or not, it was certainly *nomen et omen*, as his history at its great turning-points so remarkably proved.

CHAPTER XV.

THE CHARACTER OF JOSEPH.

IT is not well to take leave of Joseph without trying to form some estimate of so great and influential a character in its more distinctive features.

The loyalty of the lad to his father led him to use no dissimulation or concealment with regard to the evil doings of his brethren, He did not allow himself to be drawn in to share their counsels and wrong ways. Those who have had much to do with boys, or with servants, will know how very rare a thing is this feeling of honour due to father, or mother, or master, and how much moral courage it involves. It is the earliest and greatest trial of discipline and duty. This straight and trusty loyalty was as the strong keel laid down, on which the good ship was framed and gradually built up in fair proportions. This it was that won the regard and confidence of his lord in Egypt, and that made it natural to him to argue from the same principle in rebuking the graceless and corrupt woman; and to fall back on the thought : ' How *can* I do this great wickedness, and sin against God ? ' When a second time his trusty upright-ness led him into the inevitable persecution of those that *will* live godly, it became his comfort and stay ; for 'the Lord was with him, and what he did the Lord made prosper.'

The next thing is the affectionateness of his heart, which won for him the *liking* and confidence of his com-panions, alike in happiness and in trouble. And a great firmness of purpose he inherited from Abraham his great-grandfather, with a generous magnanimity and unselfish-ness of soul. His intellect was clear and energetic, and his genius that of a born administrator, like Daniel, who, so long afterwards, brought powers so similar to as vast a task at the other extremity of the imperial field of ancient times, on the Euphrates[1].

But there was more than commanding genius in Joseph, as in Daniel. Their religion underlay, and animated, and illuminated all their motive-powers. Like Enoch and Noah, they 'walked with God,' as Abraham had done.

After Joseph had become perfectly at home in the affairs and dignities of Egypt, the husband of an Egyptian lady of high position, the deputy of his Pharaoh ; with all that would make a man forsake and forget his native land ; he was so true to the God of his fathers and the covenant that He had sworn that, as Dr. Edersheim has well said : ' Instead of seeking for his

---

[1] Daniel was a prince of the other great house, the line of Judah. It is well worthy of remark that the story of this wielder of authority has been elucidated from the lore of Babylonia by Lenormant (*La Divination chez les Chaldéens*) and others, even as the narrative of Joseph's times by Ebers and the Egyptologists.

sons the honours which the court of Egypt offered them he distinctly renounced all to share the lot of the despised shepherd-race.' 'He hastened to bring his two sons, that they might be installed as co-heirs with the other sons of Jacob. In this Joseph signally showed his faith [1].' Such an one was he as those to whom St. John wrote : 'I have written unto you, young men, because ye are strong, and the word of God abideth in you, and ye have overcome the wicked one : . . . the world passeth away, and the lust thereof, but he that doeth the will of God abideth for ever [2].'

[1] *History of the Patriarchs*, vol. i. p. 178.   [2] 1 John ii. 14, 17.

APPENDICES.

—◆—

APPENDIX A.

Khamor has been taken as meaning 'he-ass;' but I doubt if, as a princely name, this is its true significance; and it seems to me that Professor Robertson Smith has not sufficient warrant in treating this name as an 'unmistakable' indication that the 'totem system' prevailed in Canaan [1].

The root has the significance of 'rising,' or being raised up, and in Assyrian the same ideograph stands for 'ass' and 'homer' (measure).

Is it not likely that the title of honour was derived independently of the name of the animal?

Among these Canaanites Jacob dwelt for the greater part of ten years, having acquired from them by purchase a possession of land for his tribe in the beautiful and watered plain.

APPENDIX B.

The great temple, which was the centre of Egyptian learning from a time long before the days of Joseph, is now utterly gone. 'The ruins of Heliopolis,' wrote Mariette, 'consist only of an immense enclosure, in the centre of which stands an obelisk.

[1] *Journal of Philology*, 1880, p. 94.

M

. . . . . As for the obelisk itself, it should be regarded with interest, for it is the oldest in Egypt. It bears, in fact, the cartouches of Usertasen I., the second king of the XIIth dynasty. It is a little more than sixty-six English feet high. Formerly a casing of copper, of pyramidal form, covered its point, which still existed in the time of Abd-el-Latyf, an Arab doctor of Bagdad, who visited Egypt about 1190 A.D.'

The fellow-obelisk, formerly standing in the front of the temple, is now entirely gone.

The great temple-enclosure measures about 4000 English feet by 3000. The sacred spring is hard by, and is hallowed by Christian tradition as the resting-place of the later Joseph and Mary with the Divine Babe of Bethlehem.

On the general subject of the viceregal office under the Hyksôs sovereigns, we must not pass over the very interesting suggestions of Mr. Flinders Petrie with regard to an altar found by him among the ruins of Tell Nebesheh—about eight miles south-east of the great and celebrated field of Sân (Zoan). This altar was originally a work of Amen-em-hat II., but bears inscriptions added by a high functionary of much later date. I quote Mr. Petrie's exposition[1]: 'They were engraved by a certain chief of the Chancellors and Royal Seal-bearer, whose name and further titles are effaced. This person was one of a series of officials whose titles were singularly parallel to the English Lord High-Chancellor, and Lord Privy Seal. Such titles imply a unique position, or one which would only be held in duplicate by a viceroy in a different province, such as the Princes of Cush under the XVIIIth dynasty. The further evidence of the power of the successive holders of this double office is seen from their having a series of scarabs, like those of the kings and members of the royal families of the XIIth and XIVth dynasties with their names and titles: many such are known.

Besides this, no other instance is known, so far as I remember,

[1] *Tell Nebesheh*, p. 16; see pl. ix. 1.

of a personage not actually reigning who has usurped royal monuments in a public temple, and even in a capital of a nome, as this
chief chancellor has appropriated the two sphinxes before mentioned, and this monument, by long inscriptions. This altar gives,
therefore, much fresh light on this obscure class of officials; it shows
that they existed after the XIIth dynasty, though of course before
the XVIIIth, and that they usurped prerogatives otherwise reserved
to reigning kings. So far, we are on certain facts. To turn now
briefly to an hypothesis suggested by these facts. We find in
the Hyksôs invasion the rule of a hated and conquering race;
yet a rule which did not at all crush out the civilization which it
already found in Egypt. Further, after a time, it gradually
imbibed the civilization over which it dominated; and yet it
was a rule without much civil organization, if any, since it was
only, as Manetho says, 'at length they made one of themselves
king,' after conquering and pillaging the country[1]. Πέρας δέ
implies finally, at the end of all the invasion, struggle, and
capture of the inhabitants. The nearest historical parallel, by
the light of which we must judge this case, is the Arab invasion
of Egypt, and subjugation of the Copts: here the conquered
were under the debasement of Byzantine rule, as the Egyptians of
the XIIIth and XIVth dynasties were living under the decayed
forms of the civilization of the Xth; but the conquerors were more
civilized probably than the Hyksôs, and more capable of organ-
izing themselves; yet we see that they adopted the arts and the
government which they found in the country to a great extent,
and—like the Hyksôs—became Egyptianized.

But one thing they took much as they found it,—the bureau-
cracy who managed all the details of the needful administration
of the country. The officials continued to be Copts, and there
was probably little break in the inherited offices of the internal
organization. Now this is exactly an explanation of what we
can see under the Hyksôs. They conquered the country as a
military horde, without even a king; they levied tribute[2], but

[1] Jos. *Cont. Ap.* I. 14.   [2] 1st *Sallier Pap.* 1. 2.

M 2

they probably had the sense to make the natives collect it for them, and left the native organization to follow its own ways. A very curious evidence of this being in after times believed to have been the case, even when the Hyksôs were as much Egyptianized as possible, is given us in the celebrated fragment of the first Sallier papyrus, which at least shows us what was the tradition of their rule. In that we find, that even for a royal letter the Hyksôs Apapi is said not to dictate his own words, but to be completely in the hands of his scribes, for 'King Apapi sent to the ruler of the South a notice, according as his scribes knowing in affairs said.' 'This view explains the continuity so evident between the middle kingdom and the rise of the empire; it exactly agrees with the one or two fragments of information that remain to us, and it accords with the historic parallel of the later invasion from Asia.'

'Now to apply the facts we have noticed above: There is a series of viziers, men who acted for the king over the treasury and taxes, and over the royal decrees, and public documents bearing the king's seal. These men lived after the XIIth and before the XVIIIth dynasty. And, further, they would seem to have acted for rulers who did not care about the public monuments, and would allow them to usurp them at their pleasure.

'Here we have the exact description of a native vizier of a Hyksôs king. We have but fragments and suggestions to lead us, but every item that we can glean exactly falls into a consistent place on this hypothesis, and would be hard to adjust to any other.

'Lieblein has already pointed out how the XIVth dynasty, with its short reigns, averaging only two years and a half, represents viceroys of the Hyksôs; but may these not be identical with the men who in the Hyksôs country were reckoned as viziers, while by their own countrymen in the upper country they were counted as kings? They may have even had a different title, and acted as viziers in one part of the country, and as semi-

independent kings in another part.   Or the viziers may have
been the lower title which the chief of the native administration
had to adopt when the Hyksôs made themselves a king.
This is a point on which we must wait for more light.'

'But yet one further document may be quoted, as giving and
receiving light on this question.   The account of Joseph in the
Book of Genesis undoubtedly refers to the Hyksôs period, and
there we read, " Let Pharaoh look out a man discreet and wise,
and set him over the land of Egypt,"—not, Let Pharaoh give
orders to his own officers.

' "And Pharaoh said unto Joseph . . . Thou shalt be over my
house, and according unto thy word shall all my people be
ruled; only in the throne will I·be greater than thou.   And
Pharaoh said unto Joseph, See, I have set thee over all the land
of Egypt.   And Pharaoh took off his signet ring from his hand,
and put it upon Joseph's hand, and arrayed him in vestures of
fine linen, and put a gold chain about his neck ; and he made
him to ride in the second chariot which he had ; and they cried
before him, Abrech; and he set him over all the land of
Egypt."   Here we read of the investiture of a vizier under the
Hyksôs, creating him royal seal-bearer, and giving him the
honour of the second chariot.   This, we now see, was not an
extraordinary act of an autocrat, but the filling up of a regular
office of the head of the native administration.'

It is not to be doubted that this extended quotation will be
welcome to the thoughtful reader.   It is taken from a learned •
memoir on recent excavations, little known except to a small
circle of Egyptologists, and it makes still more comprehensible
and natural the exaltation of Joseph to so great a responsibility
and power.

It is also very consonant with the remarkable Semitic title
Shallit bestowed upon Joseph, and identical, as elsewhere
noticed, with the title *Salatis*, assumed by the first elected king
of the Hyksôs.

It is a very remarkable thing that among the sepulchral

memorials at Abydos, described by Mariette in his important *Catalogue Général des Monuments d'Abydos*, Paris, 1880 (p. 421), are inscriptions of a Semitic foreigner who held the high office of 'First Minister of the King' in the reign of Merenptah (about the time of the Exodus). His native name was Ben-Matsana of the land of Zarbasana, but he had, as usual, a royal Egyptian name, Râmeses-em-per-Râ, with the surname Meri-An. His father's name was Iupa-â, a foreigner. This tablet belongs to 'a group of seven inhabitants of Abydos, three Egyptians, three Semites, besides a seventh personage, first minister of the king, who is of Syrian origin, and possesses two surnames, the one Egyptian, the other Semitic.'

'Let us mark,' continues Mariette, 'that with Meneptah and his minister Râmeses-em-per-Râ we are at the time of the Exodus. Let us mark that with all these names we may compare that of the Syrian Arisu (ארסו), the same whom we see, towards the end of the XIXth dynasty, puts himself at the head of the rebellion which interrupts violently the succession of the legitimate king [1]. Who knows if the Semites of our *stelæ*, or at least their sons, took part in this anti-national movement?'

APPENDIX C.

The commissariat arrangements of Joseph receive fresh light from the old standing system of victualling in the Egyptian cities, by means of strongly-guarded magazines of provisions, especially of corn, in the chief cities of the Nomes. This has been explained, and illustrated from the history of Joseph, by M. Philippe Virey in his translation of the Precepts of Ptah-hotep in the new series of *Records of the Past*, vol. iii. pp. 7–11, and previously in part in his elaborate account of the Tomb of Am-n-teh in the *Recueil de Travaux*, &c., vol. vii. p. 32 *et seqq*. We here see with what a stately perfection the system of food-

---

[1] Great Harris Papyrus.

supply was organized from the very earliest times of which we have records in Egypt.

It was no innovation on the part of Joseph, and if (as Mr. Flinders Petrie says) his office was not a novelty, neither was the administrative system by which he carried it out with such prescient success.

APPENDIX D.

On the Late Date assigned to some of the Biblical Egyptian Names.

In the *Zeitschrift für Aegyptische Sprache*, 1889, p. 41, Dr. Steindorff has treated of the names Zaphnath-pa'aneakh, Asenath, and Potipherâ, and drawn from them the conclusion that the narrative in Genesis cannot be of earlier date than the XXIInd Egyptian dynasty (the Biblical Shishak, &c.). And Brugsch has expressed a similar opinion in his recent paper published in the *Deutsche Rundschau*, May, 1890, on the ground that names of the forms in question were first used in Egypt at the period mentioned.

This of course involves a charge of anachronism which would imply a mere fiction of late date as to the new name given to Joseph, and the names assigned to his master, his father-in-law, and his wife.

I have written something in reply in the *Academy*, Jan. 31, 1891, which has not yet been answered. This is not the place for an elaborate argument, but it is right to consider so very serious a charge against the Biblical narrator, which (by the way) would equally affect the name Puti-el, given in Exodus vi. 25, as that of the father-in-law of Eleazar, the son of Aaron, whose son Phinehas (Pi-nehas) had equally an Egyptian name. We have two names of this form in Genesis and one in Exodus open to this objection.

But, without going farther, as it is easy to do, a single instance prominently adduced in an earlier work by Brugsch himself, appears to give sufficient contradiction to the late date assigned to names of this type.   It is the very notable name Pe-tu-Ba'al, contained in a stele in the Museum of the Louvre[1].   This stele, of the time of Thothmes III., contains the names of six generations of one family at Thebes, going back into or near to the times of the Hyksôs kings, as Brugsch and de Rougé and Lieblein all agree ; and the original ancestor is this very Pet-Ba'al, or Pe-tu-Ba'al, for so Brugsch himself has rendered the name 'the gift of Ba'al[2],' and Lieblein (as above cited).   It is true that the name is written in the stele as 𓊃 instead of the usual 𓂋, but we have in the *Dict. des Noms Hierog.* the pure Egyptian name 𓁐𓂋𓂧𓏤, No. 1249, which seems to warrant this conclusion.

There are classic authorities for Egyptian names of this construction of much earlier date.   But, at all events, if no such Egyptian instance had yet been found earlier than the ninth century B.C., it would be highly 'uncritical' to assume that the three instances of Potiphar, Potiphera, and Puti-el are all falsifications of late date.   Why should they not rank as evidence of the early use of names of this type at the dates to which they refer in the narrative?   Instead of this fair treatment, Brugsch has said that 'the latest redactor of Joseph's history,' who in other things proved himself, as far as knowledge of the language goes, extremely well versed in acquaintance with Egyptian matters, 'chose out for the father-in-law of his hero a name which belonged to his own time, and would refer to the sun-priest of On.'

This kind of treatment is surely unjustifiable.   It has been so proved again and again, as in the case of Sargon, and the Elam of Genesis xiv, and many instances beside.   This supposed proof of a negative from the limitation of one's own knowledge

---

[1] De Rougé, *Mons. du Louvre*, 98, Lieblein, *Recherches sur la Chronologie Egyptienne*, 129 ; *Dict. des Noms hieroglyphiques*, No. 553; Brugsch, *History* (Eng. trans.), vol. i. p. 255.

[2] *Histoire*, &c. vol. i. p. 172.

is not to be called a proof at all. It is interesting to remember that the celebrated statue of Râ-hotep at Gizeh represents a man who bore the same office as Potipherâ, as well as an almost equivalent name.

The name Pe-tu-râ (identical with Potipherâ, the article only being omitted) has been recorded by Wiedemann as belonging to the superintendent of oxen of Thothmes I., within a century of the last Hyksôs king. The author subsequently corrects the reading to Pe-en-râ (he who belongs to Râ), a very similar name to both the others.

With regard to the name given to Joseph by the Pharaoh, there are many rival explanations given by Egyptologists, and if one conjecture will only fit a late date, others will much better agree with the Hyksôs period, as we have seen. Similarly the name of Joseph's wife, אסנת, Asnat, is now explained by Steindorff as the late form Nes-Neit (belonging to [the goddess] Neit); but Brugsch himself has said 'the name of his wife Asnat is pure Egyptian, and almost entirely confined to the old and middle empire. It is derived from the very common female name Sant, or Snat[1].

I am not careful to answer such an argument as the proleptic use of the expression 'land of Râmeses.' This was in the time of Moses doubtless the familiar name of the district. If we read in an old English chronicle that Peterborough was destroyed by Norsemen in Alfred's time, we do not call this statement 'an historical-geographical error,' because the name of the place at that time was Medehamstead, and the dedication to St. Peter subsequent.

A remarkable inscription of Persian or Ptolemaic date, found by Mr. Wilbour in the island of Sehêl, high up the Nile, has led to much speculation, which may be read in Dr. Brugsch's article in the *Deutsche Rundschau*, before cited (p. 252), in the *Zeitschrift f. Aeg. Sprache*, 1890, 109, 111; and at much greater length in the former author's work *Die Biblischen Sieben Jahre*

[1] *History* (Eng. trans.). vol. i. p. 265.

der Hungersnoth, &c., Leipzig, 1891.   In this inscription there is recorded a plentiful harvest for seven years, followed by seven years of famine, and these are identified by Brugsch with those so famous in the history of Joseph.   He considers that the Biblical writer of late date brought this ancient famine into his story.   But the name of the Pharaoh in the rock-inscription, although occurring twice, is not legible in any certain sense. Brugsch and Steindorff read it in a form which they identify with the name of Tosorthros of the third dynasty.   But Professor Sayce tells me that he and Mr. Wilbour, after repeated inspections of the inscription itself, read all the three hieroglyphic signs in question quite differently from this; and the Pharaonic name can neither be certainly read nor (of course) identified.

Under these circumstances it is idle to insist upon any particular date for these years of plenty and famine, and, although the monumental record of them is very highly interesting, we cannot tell in what relation it stands to the narrative of the administration of Joseph; and there is no need to attach any degree of importance to the assumption that it is the Egyptian version of the 'Genesis-legend,' which Brugsch assigns to the time of the XXVIth dynasty, known to Bible-students by the Pharaohs Neko and Hophra.

APPENDIX E.

The Egyptian Queens Mût-em-ua and Teie.

In an address to the British Association at Manchester, and in a paper published in the *Journal of the Anthropological Institute* (1888), I have given reasons for the conjecture that Mût-em-ua, the mother of the celebrated Amenhotep III., and grandmother of the 'heretic king' Amenhotep IV. (Khu-en-aten), was a princess of Pûn (South-west Arabia and Somâli-land).   But it now appears from the Tel-el-Amarna tablets that this queen was the daughter of a king of Mitanni (a Mesopotamian kingdom opposite to Karkemish).

With regard to the well-favoured royal lady Teie, wife of Amenhotep IV., Professor Sayce has inferred from a passage in one of the Tel-el-Amarna tablets that she was a daughter of Burraburyas, king of Babylonia. This has since been doubted, but Professor Sayce does not see any other way of understanding the passage, which he renders thus: 'Translation of the letter from Teie (No. 188) so far as the text is clear and unbroken :—" To my son (*bini*, the Canaanite word, not the Assyrian *abil*), speaks thus the daughter of the king : To thyself, thy chariots [thy horses, &c.] may there be peace! May the gods of Burra-buryas go with thee ! I go in peace .... Here .... a tablet (= letter) from .... My messenger has brought silver to thy city-fortress, and may thy .... be at peace!" .... then comes the following postscript: "Thy servant Kidin-Hadad accomplishes (the errand) : may my lord go (= live) for ever!" '

We may hope to know more of this interesting queen, and of the disk-worship, so short-lived as it was in Egypt. With regard to physiognomy it is of course possible, as far as we know, that, otherwise than through her father, Mût-em-ua may have been of Pûnite descent.

LIST OF SCRIPTURE REFERENCES.

INDEX.

THE END.

www.ingramcontent.com/pod-product-compliance
Lightning Source LLC
Chambersburg PA
CBHW030603040726
47497CB00008B/2829